Volume **1** # THE GOLDEN BOOK ENCYCLOPEDIA

Aaron to antiseptic

aa-an

An exciting, up-to-date encyclopedia in 20 fact-filled, entertaining volumes

Especially designed as a first encyclopedia for today's grade-school children

More than 2,500 full-color photographs and illustrations

From the Publishers of Golden® Books

Western Publishing Company, Inc.
Racine, Wisconsin 53404

ILLUSTRATION CREDITS
(t=top, b=bottom, c=center, l=left, r=right)

1 Susan McCartney/Photo Researchers; 7 t. David Lindroth Inc.; 7 bl. Focus on Sports: 8 tl. Laurie Bender; 8 br. Noren Trotman/Sports Chrome; 9. Penny Tweedie/Woodfin Camp: 10 bl. Oscar® statuette. © Academy of Motion Picture Arts and Sciences®: 10 br. *Simple Things*© 1952 The Walt Disney Company; 11 tr. Tom Powers/Joseph. Mindlin & Mulvey; 11 br. Richard Hutchings; 12 tl. William Hubbell/Woodfin Camp; 12 tr. R. Vroom/ Miller Services Ltd./Photo Researchers; 13. Susan McCartney/Photo Researchers; 14 both. Courtesy of Dick Smith; 15 tl. Bryce Flynn/Picture Group; 15 br and inset. *Mrs. John Adams* and *John Adams*, Gilbert Stuart, National Gallery of Art, Washington, D.C., gift of Mrs. Robert Homans; 16 br. Brown Brothers; 16 inset. Bettmann Archive; 17 American Cancer Society; 18. Marcus Hamilton; 19. Tom Powers/Joseph. Mindlin & Mulvey; 20. Richard Hutchings; 21 tl. David Lindroth Inc.; 21 tr. © Joe Viesti; 22. Harold C. Kinne/Photo Researchers; 23 tl. Marc & Evelyne Bernheim/Woodfin Camp; 23 tr. David Lindroth Inc.; 23 c. Thomas Nebbia/Woodfin Camp; 25 t. David Lindroth Inc.; 25 bl. Bridgeman Art Library/Art Resource; 26. Marc & Evelyne Bernheim/Woodfin Camp; 27 bl. Alon Reininger/Woodfin Camp; 27 br. J. Guichard/Sygma; 28. Marc & Evelyne Bernheim/Woodfin Camp; 29. Diane Rawson/Photo Researchers; 30-31. Marilyn Bass; 32. Bill Hilton; 33. Lloyd P. Birmingham; 34-35. Tom LaPadula/Evelyne Johnson Associates; 36. David R. Frazier/Photo Researchers; 37. Brian Sullivan; 38. George Hall/Woodfin Camp; 39. Tom Powers/Joseph, Mindlin & Mulvey; 41 tr. Marilyn Bass; 41 br. Alabama Bureau of Tourism & Travel; 43 bl. Alaska Division of Tourism; 43 br. Marilyn Bass; 45 bl. David Lindroth Inc.; 45 t. Canadian Consulate General; 46. Lois & George Cox/Bruce Coleman, Inc.; 48 b. Robert Harding Picture Library; 49. Bettmann Archive; 52. Michael O'Reilly/Joseph, Mindlin & Mulvey; 53 tl. Adam Woolfitt/Woodfin Camp; 53 tr. David Lindroth Inc.; 54. Neil Leifer/Alskog/Photo Researchers; 55 br. Dennis O'Brien/Joseph. Mindlin & Mulvey; 56. John Hamberger/Lillian Flowers; 57 b. John Hamberger/Lillian Flowers; 58 br. Richard Hutchings; 58 inset. American Numismatic Society, New York; 59. *The World Almanac & Book of Facts*, 1987 edition. copyright © Newspaper Enterprise Association. Inc., 1986. New York, N.Y. 10166; 61. David Lindroth Inc.; 62 tl. Paolo Koch/Photo Researchers; 63 both, Michael Abbey/Science Source/Photo Researchers; 64-67. Marcus Hamilton; 72-73. Fiona Reid/Artist Network; 73 c. Karl Ammann/Bruce Coleman, Inc.; 74. John C. Hutchins; 75 bl. Fiona Reid/Artist Network; 75 br. Jeff Foott/Tom Stack & Associates; 76 both. John Rice/Joseph. Mindlin & Mulvey; 77. Tom Brakefield/Bruce Coleman, Inc.; 78-79 b. Dennis O'Brien/Joseph. Mindlin & Mulvey; 79 t. John Hamberger/Lillian Flowers; 80. Ron Cohn/ The Gorilla Foundation; 81 both. John Rice/Joseph. Mindlin & Mulvey; 82. John Hamberger; 83 bl. Smithsonian Institution; 83 br. John Hamberger/Lillian Flowers; 84. John Hamberger/Lillian Flowers; 85 t. John Hamberger/Lillian Flowers; 86. Richard Thom/Tom Stack & Associates; 87. John Hamberger/Lillian Flowers and Fiona Reid/Artist Network; 88. Wally McNamee/Woodfin Camp; 89. Dennis O'Brien/Joseph. Mindlin & Mulvey; 90 tl. George Holton/Photo Researchers; 90 tr. NSF/Russ Kinne/Photo Researchers; 90 inset. Michael O'Reilly/Joseph. Mindlin & Mulvey; 91. David Lindroth Inc.; 92 br. Historical Pictures Service. Inc., Chicago; 92 t. John Hamberger/Lillian Flowers; 92 inset. U.S. Mint; 93. Tom McHugh/California Academy of Sciences/Photo Researchers; 94 tl. Marc & Evelyne Bernheim/Woodfin Camp; 94 bl. Michal Heron/Woodfin Camp; 94 br. R. Rowan/Photo Researchers; 96. Harriet Phillips/Lillian Flowers.

COVER CREDITS
Center: Susan McCartney/Photo Researchers. Clockwise from top: Oscar® Statuette © Academy of Motion Picture Arts and Sciences®; John Hamberger/Lillian Flowers; Focus on Sports; Harriet Phillips/Lillian Flowers; Brian Sullivan; David Lindroth Inc.

Library of Congress Catalog Card Number: 87-82741
ISBN: 0-307-70101-8

ABCDEFGHIJKL

WELCOME TO
THE GOLDEN BOOK ENCYCLOPEDIA

Did you know that a whale can live to be 70 years old?

Did you know that one grain of salt has 20 million billion atoms?

Did you know that the largest dinosaur weighed 80 tons and stood as tall as a six-story building?

These are only a few of the thousands of amazing and interesting facts you will find in the *Golden Book Encyclopedia*. Through its exciting pages, you will get a closer look at the world around you. The 20 lively volumes are filled with clear, easy-to-understand articles and thousands of dramatic and colorful photographs, illustrations, maps, charts, and diagrams. This encyclopedia has been designed especially for you—to make learning an adventure!

Explore the pages of your *Golden Book Encyclopedia*. Look up things you are interested in. Or just page through a volume, discovering amazing and unexpected facts.

Use the *Golden Book Encyclopedia* to learn more about interesting subjects you discuss in school. Look at entries such as **animal, computer, sports,** or **weather.** Look for a state or foreign country you are studying. Make the *Golden Book Encyclopedia* your partner when doing school projects or homework.

There are so many interesting things to learn! The *Golden Book Encyclopedia* provides a rich beginning, offering important facts about many subjects. The information in the *Golden Book Encyclopedia* can give you a head start in learning. It can be a stepping-stone to other books and materials about subjects that are exciting to you. In addition, it can become a center of fun and learning for your whole family.

The Editors

HOW TO USE
THE GOLDEN BOOK ENCYCLOPEDIA

Every day, there are times when you want to know more about something. Sometimes you can ask a parent or a teacher. But sometimes you need more information than they can give. The *Golden Book Encyclopedia* can tell you more about many different subjects. You can find out about places in the world, about plants and animals, about people, and about many other subjects. It is easy to use, so you can look up information by yourself.

The *Golden Book Encyclopedia* has more than 1,900 pages in 20 volumes! To find things easily, you need to know how it is arranged.

In an encyclopedia, there are many short articles about different subjects. Each article begins with an *entry heading* that looks like this:

alligators and crocodiles

The entry headings are arranged in alphabetical order. All the entries beginning with *A* are in the first two volumes. All the entries beginning with *Z* are in the very last volume. In the *A*s, the very first entry starts with the letters *aa*. Then come the entries starting with *ab*, then *ac*, and so on.

Sometimes the encyclopedia gives you a "road sign," telling you where to look for the information you want. For example, if you look up **crocodile,** you will find an entry heading, but no information. Instead, you will see,

crocodile, *see* alligators and crocodiles

This is called a *cross-reference.* It tells you that you will find information about crocodiles if you look up the entry **alligators and crocodiles.**

When you are reading an entry, sometimes you will find other cross-references. For example, there is a cross-reference at the end of the entry on **alligators and crocodiles.** It says,

See also **reptile.**

This tells you that you may learn more about alligators and crocodiles and animals like them if you look up **reptile.** Sometimes you may look up a word and find no entry or cross reference. What can you do then? Go to the **index** in volume 20. For example, if you look up **gavial** in the encyclopedia, you won't find an entry or a cross-reference. But if you look up **gavial** in the index, it will say this:

gavial, 1:57

This tells you that if you look in volume 1 on page 57, you will find out something about a gavial. When you read that page, you will learn that a gavial is an animal related to alligators and crocodiles.

The *Golden Book Encyclopedia* also provides guides to pronouncing some difficult words. For example, an entry in volume 1 is **aborigine.** When the word first appears in the text, it is spelled a special way in parentheses—(ab-uh-RIJ-uh-nee). This tells you how the word should sound. The part of the word in capital letters is the part that gets the stress.

The *Golden Book Encyclopedia* is useful for looking up information. But it is also fun to look through. If there isn't any one thing you want to look up, just wander from page to page. You will soon be sure to find something that interests you. No matter what you are interested in, the *Golden Book Encyclopedia* can help you learn more about it.

The Editors

CONSULTANTS AND CONTRIBUTORS

Barbara Branca, M.A.. author of science textbooks and science books for young readers: former science teacher.

Karen Breen, M.L.S.. Children's Services Consultant. Queensborough Public Library. New York. New York.

Harris Burstin, M.D.. Assistant Professor of Pediatrics. New York University School of Medicine.

Bettye Caldwell, Ph.D.. Donaghey Distinguished Professor of Education. University of Arkansas at Little Rock.

Kenneth W. Dowling, Ph.D.. Supervisor of Science Education. State of Wisconsin.

Eden Force Eskin, B.A.. writer. editor. lexicographer: textbook author and editor: author of *Theodore Roosevelt* (for young readers).

Fernando U. Fajardo, B.S.. consulting chemical engineer and writer on chemistry for reference books.

Paula Franklin, B.A.. author of *Indians of North America* and *Our Nation's Constitution;* coauthor of *A History of the United States* and *Comprehensive United States History.*

Betty L. Glennon, M.S.. elementary teacher. reading specialist. instructor in gifted and talented programs. author and editor of books and workbooks for young readers.

Kathryn A. Goldner, B.A.. writer. editor. former teacher. coauthor of *Why Mount St. Helens Blew Its Top. Humphrey the Wrong-Way Whale,* and numerous science articles.

Marcia Golub, B.A.. writer and editor: contributor to reference books on literature and language.

Paul Heacock, B.A.. writer and editor: author of *Webster's Spell It Right Dictionary* and *Which Word When?*

Alice Jones, B.A.. elementary teacher. Ligonier Valley School District. Ligonier. Pennsylvania.

Sharon Kahkonen, M.S.. M.A.T.. writer and editor of science textbooks. articles. and stories for young readers.

Robert Kelley, Ed.D.. Instructor in Physics. Skidmore College: former Supervisor for Physics and Earth Science. State of New York.

Douglas A. Lancaster, Ph.D.. Associate Professor of Biology. Mercy College: former editor of Cornell University's *The Living Bird;* consultant on the *Audubon Society Encyclopedia of North American Birds.*

Peter Margolin, B.A.. contributor of earth-science articles to four encyclopedias and Senior Science Editor of the *Random House Unabridged Dictionary.*

Ann Whipple Marr, M.A.. teacher of mathematics and computer science: writer.

Janet McHugh, B.S.. contributor to history books for young readers: former social-studies textbook editor.

Paul Miller, M.B.A.. Director of Institutional Research. Midstate College. Peoria. Illinois.

Sarah Myers, Ph.D.. former director of the American Geographical Society and editor of *Geographical Review.*

Peter Oliver, B.A.. contributor to magazines for young readers: recipient of award for excellence in educational writing from the Educational Press Association of America.

Robert Orsi, Ph.D.. Professor of Religious Studies. Fordham University.

David Price, M.A.. anthropologist at the University of Florida. Gainesville: coauthor. teacher's edition of *Cultural Anthropology* by Marvin Harris.

Karin L. Rhines, M.A.. author of science textbooks: former member of the Biological Sciences Curriculum Study Group. Boulder. Colorado.

Marc Sacerdote, M.A.. teacher and program developer of film animation for the New York City schools: contributing author/editor of science and mathematics articles for reference books and texts.

William E. Shapiro, M.A.. Executive Editor. *Worldmark Encyclopedia of the Nations;* former Editor in Chief. the *New Book of Knowledge.*

Jenny Tesar, M.S.. author of *Parents as Teachers, Introduction to Animals,* and *Disney's Wonders of Wildlife* series: Senior Editor. the *Illustrated Encyclopedia of the Animal Kingdom.*

Tina Thoburn, Ed.D.. coauthor. the *Golden Picture Dictionary;* senior author of popular elementary mathematics and English language-arts textbook series.

William Travis, Ed.D.. Director of Curriculum. K–12. Pittsfield Public Schools. Pittsfield. Massachusetts.

Carole G. Vogel, M.A.T.. writer. editor. former teacher. coauthor of *Why Mount St. Helens Blew Its Top. Humphrey the Wrong-Way Whale,* and numerous science articles.

Bruce Wetterau, author of the *Macmillan Concise Dictionary of World History* and of many science articles.

Helen Wright, M.L.S.. Assistant Director of Publishing Services. and Interim Director of Library Outreach Services. American Library Association: contributor to the *Encyclopedia of Library and Information Sciences* and *New Book of Knowledge.*

STAFF

For Western Publishing Company

Administrative and Financial Director: John F. Harris
Editorial Director: Patricia A. Reynolds
Editorial Production Administrator: JoAnn Nicholson
Litho Production Manager: Ray Auchter
Type and Composition: Datapage Division
    Joan Mersch. Account Manager

For Macmillan Educational Company

Editor in Chief: Lawrence T. Lorimer
Science Editor: Bryan H. Bunch
Copy Chief: Veronica F. Towers
Editorial Staff: Diana Perez. Alexa Ripley Barre. Kathleen Derzipilski. Carolyn Krinsley. Carl Johnes. Kim Barker. Thomas Quash. Michael Elkan
Art Direction: Pam Forde Graphics
Photo Editor: Elnora Bode
Cartographic Consultant: David Lindroth
Art Staff: Laurie Bender. Rachelle Engelman Friedle. Kathleen Marks
Cover Art Direction: Raúl Rodriguez

In the picture writing of the ancient Egyptians, the letter *A* looked like the head of an ox.

The Phoenicians and early Hebrews called it *aleph,* meaning "ox."

The Greeks called it *alpha.* It looked almost like our capital *A.*

Aaron, Henry

Henry ("Hank") Aaron was one of the greatest baseball players who ever played the game. He hit more home runs in his career than any other major leaguer. Other players were flashier than Hank Aaron, yet very few accomplished as much.

Aaron was born in Mobile, Alabama, in 1934. In 1954, when he was 20 years old, he joined the Milwaukee Braves of the National League. Aaron played in the major leagues for 23 years. He never broke any records for a single season, but he was a steady, reliable hitter. In 18 different seasons, he hit 25 or more home runs. In all, he came to bat more than 12,000 times, got more than 3,700 hits, and scored more than 2,000 runs. His greatest achievement was hitting 755 home runs, an all-time major-league record.

Home-run champion Hank Aaron swings at the baseball.

In 1974, Aaron was still playing for the Braves, now called the Atlanta Braves. That spring, he tied Babe Ruth's record of 714 home runs. Fans waited for him to hit one more homer and break the record. When he hit his 715th homer, the game was stopped and there was a big celebration. Millions watched on television and cheered Aaron's new record. President Gerald Ford called to congratulate him.

Hank Aaron retired from baseball in 1977. Five years later, he was elected to baseball's Hall of Fame.

See also **baseball.**

abacus

An abacus is a very simple calculator. A person can count, add, subtract, multiply, and divide on an abacus by moving beads.

The abacus was developed thousands of years ago. The earliest abacus was a board covered with sand or dust. Marks made in the sand or dust were used in place of numbers. In fact, the word *abacus* comes from a word meaning "dust."

The modern abacus has rows of rods or wires inside a frame. Beads that can be moved up and down are strung on the rods. Each rod has a place value. The beads represent numbers. The rod farthest to the right is the ones position. On this rod, each bead below the middle bar is worth 1. Each bead above the middle bar is worth 5. The next rod is the tens position. Each bead below the bar is worth 10, and each bead above is worth 50. The third rod is the hundreds

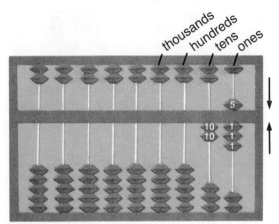

The abacus shows the number 28—
one 5 and three 1s in the right row,
and two 10s in the next row.

position. Each bead below the bar is worth 100, and each bead above the bar is worth 500. The next rod is the thousands position, and so on. To show a number, you move the beads toward the middle bar.

With practice, an abacus is easy to use. To add 7 to 16, for example, first show 16 on the abacus by pushing a one-bead, a five-bead, and a ten-bead toward the middle bar. Then add 7 by moving the second five-bead and two more one-beads toward the middle. Exchange the two five-beads for a ten-bead, and there is the answer: 23.

Different kinds of abacuses are used in many parts of the world. Students in China and Japan do their arithmetic with abacuses. In the Soviet Union, a shopkeeper is more likely to use an abacus at the checkout counter than a cash register.

See also computer; arithmetic; and mathematics.

Abdul-Jabbar, Kareem

At 7 feet 2 inches tall, Kareem Abdul-Jabbar would stand out in any crowd. But he is special for more than his height. He made basketball history.

He was born with the name Lew Alcindor in New York City in 1947. In junior high school, he was already tall for his age. At 17, he was considered the best high-school player in the country. In 1965, Alcindor went to the University of California at Los Angeles (UCLA). He was a good student. He also helped UCLA win the national basketball championship three times in four years.

In 1969, Alcindor joined the Milwaukee Bucks of the National Basketball Association (NBA). The Bucks were one of the league's worst teams when he arrived. Only a year later, they won the NBA championship.

Alcindor became a follower of the religion Islam. He took the Muslim name Kareem Abdul-Jabbar in 1971. He continued to play well. Traded to the Los Angeles Lakers in 1975, he led his new team to three NBA championships. Abdul-Jabbar was chosen the league's most valuable player six times.

Scoring champ Kareem Abdul-Jabbar.

In 1984, Abdul-Jabbar became basketball's greatest scorer ever. He broke the record of 31,419 points set by Wilt Chamberlain. After that, every basket he made set a new record. Kareem Abdul-Jabbar will be first in the record books for years to come.

See also basketball.

abolition, *see* Civil War; Lincoln, Abraham; slavery

Ancestors of these aborigines moved to Australia many centuries ago.

aborigines

The word *aborigine* (ab-uh-RIJ-uh-nee) comes from the Latin words meaning "from the beginning." Aborigines are the first people to live in any particular place. But we usually use the word to refer to the first people to live in Australia. Australian aborigines are dark-skinned people who usually have black hair.

When Europeans first arrived in Australia in the 1700s, there were about 300,000 aborigines. Today, there are about 50,000.

Aborigines are now Australian citizens, and most work on farms or ranches. Their early way of life was very different. They lived as nomads, moving from one place to another. They hunted wild animals and gathered plants. Aborigines could not settle in one place. If they did, they would use up the food supply there. (*See* **nomad.**)

Because much of Australia is hot desert, aborigines needed many skills to survive. Aborigine men were good at hunting. They invented the boomerang, a curved stick for throwing at targets. The stick circles back to the thrower if it misses. Women were skilled at finding plants, nuts, insects, and small animals for food.

The aborigines did not own many things, because they had to carry all their possessions every time they moved. They slept in small huts called *wurleys*, made of bark and branches, and they wore only waistbands and ornaments.

Each person belonged to a large family and to an even larger tribe. There were rules for individuals, for particular families, and for particular tribes. These rules regulated such things as who could marry whom and who could do certain jobs.

There were people called "clever men" who, the aborigines believed, had unusual powers. Clever men served as doctors, interpreted dreams, and predicted the future.

The aborigines never developed a system of writing. All their knowledge was passed from one generation to the next in songs, chants, and stories.

Abraham

Abraham is the father of the Jewish and Muslim peoples. His story is told in the Book of Genesis, the first book of the Bible. Jews, Christians, and Muslims admire Abraham as a man who obeyed God.

God came to Abraham and told him to take his family to a strange country, called Canaan. Abraham had never been there, but God promised to show Abraham where to build a house. God also promised to take care of Abraham and his family.

Leaving home in search of this new land was a risky thing for Abraham to do. What if he could not find Canaan? What if his people could not live there in peace? He went anyway, because he trusted God.

Abraham did find Canaan, and he led his people into the new land. Then God made a covenant—a special agreement—with Abraham. He gave Abraham the new land and promised to help Abraham's children and grandchildren. In return, Abraham promised that he and his children would love God and live as God wanted them to live.

Abraham's descendants were the ancient Israelites, whose history is told in the Bible.

See also **Israelites; Islam; Judaism;** and **Bible.**

Academy Award

One of the biggest shows of the year in America is the Academy Awards ceremony. Famous movie stars and television personalities gather at a large theater in Los Angeles, California. Millions watch the show on television at home. They all want to know which movie has won the award as best movie of the year, and which actors and actresses have won awards for their performances.

The Academy Awards are given by the Academy of Motion Picture Arts and Sciences. The academy began in 1927 in Hollywood, a part of Los Angeles. Movies were only black-and-white back then, and had no sound. Even so, movies were popular, and many people were busy making them in Hollywood. The first members of the academy wanted to reward the people who did the best work. At the first ceremony, 11 awards were handed out at a small dinner.

Today, about 4,000 important people who help make movies are members of the academy. All the members vote to decide which movies and which people should win awards. They give other awards besides those for best picture and best actor and actress. A list of some of the awards given each year is in the box above.

Academy Awards
are given for the best work done in movies that were first shown during the previous year. They include awards for

- Best Picture
- Best Director
- Best Actor
- Best Actress
- Best Supporting Actor
- Best Supporting Actress
- Best Foreign Film
- Best Original Song
- Best Original Screenplay
- Best Cinematography (camera work)
- Best Art Director
- Best Costume Design
- Best Animated Short (cartoon)
- Best Sound
- Best Sound Effects

Each winner of an Academy Award receives a gold-plated statue of a man standing on a spool of film. The statue stands 13 inches (33 centimeters) high. In 1931, a secretary at the academy library looked at the statue and said, "He reminds me of my uncle Oscar." Soon, everyone was calling the statue Oscar. Today, the Academy Awards themselves are often called Oscars.

The Oscar was the first of all the show-business awards, and is still the most famous one.

See also **actors and acting** and **movie.**

Below, an "Oscar." Walt Disney received a special Oscar for creating Mickey Mouse, right.

acids and bases

Many common chemicals can be classified as acids or bases. Weak acids taste sour, and weak bases have a bitter taste. Sour milk, lemon juice, and vinegar all taste sour because they contain weak acids. *CAUTION: Strong acids and bases can severely burn the skin. You should never taste or touch them.*

One safe way to tell acids from bases is to use *litmus paper.* This special kind of paper turns colors when touched by a liquid acid or base. A liquid that turns blue litmus paper red is an acid. A liquid that changes red litmus paper blue is a base. Water is neutral. It does not change the color of either red or blue litmus paper.

All acids and bases can be dissolved in water. Adding water makes an acid or a base burn less and become more neutral. If you mix an acid and a base together, they cancel each other out and form a new material, called a *salt.*

We have a strong acid, hydrochloric acid, in our stomachs. It helps us to digest the foods we swallow. One reason it doesn't hurt us is that the water we drink makes the acid weaker. Another reason is that the stomach lining is made of materials the acid cannot hurt. Sulfuric acid is another strong acid. It is used in car batteries to make electricity. Weak acids, such as vinegar, are used for cooking and sometimes for cleaning. The weak acid in ketchup can remove stains from a copper-bottom pan.

Hydrogen atoms are what make an acid an acid. One molecule of hydrochloric acid has one hydrogen atom (H) joined to one atom of chlorine (Cl). So the chemical formula for hydrochloric acid is HCl. A molecule of sulfuric acid has two atoms of hydrogen joined to a group of atoms called a *sulfate* group—one atom of sulfur joined to four of oxygen (SO_4). So the chemical formula for sulfuric acid is H_2SO_4.

In a base, each molecule has a *hydroxide* group, which is an oxygen atom attached to

When you mix baking soda and lemon juice, the mixture fizzes. The bubbles are made of carbon dioxide.

a hydrogen atom (OH). In a molecule of sodium hydroxide, one sodium atom is attached to a hydroxide group. The chemical symbol for sodium is Na, so the chemical formula for sodium hydroxide is NaOH.

Sodium hydroxide and potassium hydroxide are strong bases used to unplug clogged drains and to make soaps. Ammonium hydroxide is a weak base used for cleaning glasses and mirrors.

See also **chemistry.**

When red litmus paper is dipped in a base, it turns blue.

Below are the ruins of the Parthenon, a temple built on the Acropolis in Athens. The carvings at right were once part of a temple on the Acropolis. Now they are kept in a museum in Athens, where they are protected from damage by weather or pollution.

Acropolis

Acropolis (uh-KRAHP-uh-lus) is a Greek word that means "high part of the city." The most famous Acropolis is part of the city of Athens, in Greece. During the 400s B.C. (more than 2,400 years ago), the people of Athens built several beautiful temples on their Acropolis. Today, the temples are in ruins. But every year tourists and students come from all over the world to visit and study them.

The Acropolis is a steep hill about 200 feet (61 meters) high. Before the 400s B.C., the hill was a fortress. The people of the town could take refuge there when enemies attacked. Later, the Athenians built walls around their city and no longer needed a hill fortress. They decided to build great temples on the hill instead.

Today, visitors can reach the top of the hill by climbing winding steps cut into stone. An entrance gate called the Propylaea is at the top of the stairs. Beyond the gate, there once stood a giant bronze statue of Athena. She was the Greek goddess of wisdom, and the city of Athens was named for her. The statue disappeared centuries ago.

The biggest temple on the Acropolis is the Parthenon. It was built in honor of Athena Parthenos (which means "Athena the Virgin"). It has a rectangular shape, with 8 columns along each end and 15 along each side. Inside, there was once a gold and ivory statue of Athena. Like the giant bronze statue, it has disappeared.

The Parthenon had a roof with two slanted sides, so that there was a triangular space underneath it at each end. This space, called a *pediment,* was filled with carvings of gods and goddesses. They were well planned for the space, with figures lying down at the ends and standing up in the middle. The carvings were painted red, gold, and blue.

The Parthenon also has an inner border of carvings, called a *frieze.* It shows a procession of Athenians, including men on horseback, young women, and priests leading animals for sacrifice.

Another well-known building on the Acropolis is a temple called the Erechtheum. One part that still stands is the Porch of the Maidens. Its roof is held up by marble figures of six standing women, wearing the graceful robes of ancient Greece.

See also **Greece, ancient.**

actors and acting

When you see a movie, play, or television show, you are watching a story being performed by actors. (A woman or girl actor is often called an *actress.*)

Actors play the parts of different characters in a story. Actors may not be anything like the people they are pretending to be. Good actors, however, can convince you that they are those people, and that the story characters are real.

How Actors Work Actors usually act out a play or film script that someone has written. The author writes the *dialogue*—what each character says. The author may also suggest how the character behaves. Each actor must memorize the lines of dialogue spoken by his or her character. If actors can't remember their lines, the audience watching the show won't believe the characters are real.

To seem real, actors can't just say their lines. They also have to convince an audience that they believe what they are saying.

They do this by showing the feelings their characters should be feeling. When an actor plays a happy woman, her face will look happy, and her voice will sound happy. Even the way she walks will be bouncy. All this will make the audience believe she is the happy woman whose part she is playing.

Actors also use props, costumes, and makeup to make characters seem more real. Props are things actors use or carry while they are acting. An actor playing the part of a wise old man might use a cane, a rocking chair, and a pipe as props. His costume would be an old man's clothes. He would also use makeup to make his hair gray or white and to draw wrinkles on his face.

To play a young man, the same actor might carry a portable radio and wear a T-shirt, blue jeans, and sneakers. If he had any wrinkles on his face, he could hide them with makeup.

History There have been actors for more than 2,000 years. The ancient Greeks put on plays. In each of their plays, they used only three actors to play all the parts. There was

These child actors perform in a musical in New York City. There are special schools for young performers who work every night.

a *chorus*—a group of people on stage who told the audience what was going on. The actors wore masks and costumes to play the different parts, changing whenever a new character appeared. All the actors and members of the chorus were men.

Even in the early 1600s, when the plays of William Shakespeare were first performed, no women were allowed to be actors. The parts of women and girls were acted by young men and boys. The actors used fewer props and less makeup than actors use now, but they wore complicated costumes.

For many years, most people believed that actors were bad people. This may be because actors traveled a lot from town to town to put on their plays. It may also be because they usually worked at night, when most people were home with their families. In the last 100 years, however, people have come to admire actors. Some actors help raise money for good causes. A few have become important leaders.

Acting Today Since the invention of movies in the 1890s, acting has changed a lot. Acting used to be done only in theaters, where the audience was far away. Actors had to have strong voices and make large movements so that everyone in the theater would know what was going on. In movies and television, the camera brings the actors much closer to the audience. This means that the makeup and props must look very real and

This actor covers his own hair, then uses a wig and makeup to make himself look older.

natural. The actors must move and speak naturally, too.

Universities now offer courses in acting, and there are special schools for actors. Acting teachers often have their own ideas about how to act. In some cases, actors may even *improvise*—make up their own plays as they go along.

There are many different places where actors can act. For actors who want to work in live plays, New York City is the most important place in the United States. Part of the year, actors can find parts with summer stock companies, which are groups that put on plays in summer-vacation towns.

Other actors work in movies or on television shows. Many of these are made in or near Hollywood, California. Actors may also make commercials for television, or teach acting.

Still, an actor's life is not easy. There are many more people who want to be actors than there are parts in plays and movies. If an actor does get a job, it may last for only a few weeks or months. When the show is over, the actors are out of work. Then they have to try out for parts in other shows. Many actors have other jobs when they don't have acting jobs.

acupuncture

Acupuncture is a treatment to help reduce pain. It has been used in China for more than 2,000 years to treat pain from arthritis, headaches, and many other illnesses. Chinese surgeons often use acupuncture during operations instead of giving patients an anesthetic drug. Today, some doctors in the United States use acupuncture, too. (*See* **anesthetic.**)

Acupuncturists use very thin needles about the thickness of a hair. They stick them a short way into a patient's skin and twist them quickly. Patients say this feels like getting stung by an insect. But they also say that the treatment with the needles can reduce their pain or even make it go away.

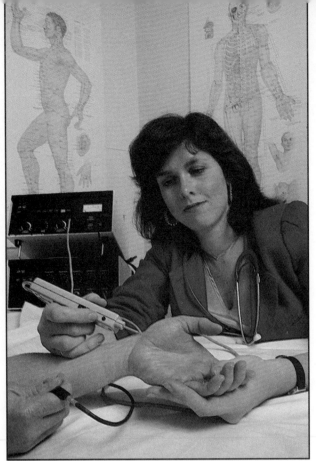

This doctor is using an electrical "wand" instead of needles to relieve pain.

An important part of acupuncture treatment is knowing exactly where the needles should be placed. The Chinese have described at least 800 locations where the needles can be used. Each spot controls pain in a specific area of the body.

Some scientists believe that acupuncture needles send messages along the nerves to the brain, telling it to release chemicals that block pain messages. But no one is sure just how acupuncture really works.

Adams family

The Adams family of Massachusetts is one of the most remarkable families in American history. It produced a leading patriot, two presidents of the United States, and many other leaders in government, law, business, and learning.

Samuel Adams The first of the Adams family important in America was Samuel. Born in 1722, he became a political leader in Massachusetts. This colony was arguing with Britain over taxes. Sam Adams wrote newspaper articles urging the colonists to stand up for their rights. In 1773, he helped organize the Boston Tea Party to protest a British tax on tea. (*See* **Boston Tea Party.**)

Sam Adams later represented his state in the two Continental Congresses. At these meetings, the problems with Britain were discussed by men from all the colonies. The Second Continental Congress declared independence from Britain, partly because of Samuel Adams's arguments. Adams was one of the first to favor war against Britain.

John Adams Sam Adams had a younger cousin, John Adams, who also supported war against Britain. Born in 1735, John Adams became the first ambassador to Britain once the United States was formed. When George Washington was chosen as the first U.S. president, John Adams became the first vice president. In 1796, he became the second president of the United States. During Adams's term of office, the capital of the

John Adams was the second president of the United States. He and his wife, Abigail, were the first family to live in the White House.

United States was moved from Philadelphia to Washington, D.C. He was the first president to live in the White House. As president, Adams's main goal was to keep the United States out of European wars.

Abigail Smith Adams When John Adams was away from home—sometimes for many months—his wife, Abigail, ran their farm in Massachusetts and raised their four children. Abigail Adams was one of the most influential women of her time. She wrote many letters to her husband, filled with news about the family and about Massachusetts. We still read these letters. They tell much about what life was like during and after the Revolution.

John Quincy Adams When John Adams traveled to Britain, he took his oldest son, John Quincy Adams, with him. John Quincy, born in 1767, was his father's assistant. He later became an important political leader himself. In 1824, he became the sixth president of the United States. John Adams and John Quincy Adams are the only father and son who were both U.S. presidents.

JQA, as John Quincy was called, was president for one term. Then he was elected to Congress. During his 17 years in Congress, he fought to end slavery in the United States.

John Quincy's son, Charles Francis, also became a congressman. Like his grandfather John, he served as ambassador to Britain. During the Civil War, Charles Adams persuaded the British not to help the South. Charles Francis's sons and other descendants of the Adams family contributed much to American learning and public life.

See also **presidents of the United States.**

---

adaptation to environment, *see* **evolution; biome**

Addams, Jane

Jane Addams spent her life helping others. She worked for the poor and for people who

could not find jobs. She helped thousands of people, especially women and children.

Jane Addams was born in Cedarville, Illinois, in 1860. From early childhood, Jane knew that she wanted to do some special work to help others. She went to medical school, but poor health forced her to drop out. Then, on a trip to London in 1888, she visited a settlement house—a place where poor people could come to receive help.

The next year, she and her friend Ellen Gates Starr bought a run-down house in Chicago. They made it a neighborhood center called Hull House. Working mothers left their children there during the day. Immigrants came to classes to learn English.

Jane Addams tried to make governments treat the poor more fairly. She worked for laws to protect children and working women. She also joined campaigns to get women the right to vote and to promote peace among the countries of the world.

In 1931, Jane Addams received the Nobel Prize for peace. She died in 1935.

Jane Addams, at right, started nurseries where working mothers could leave their children.

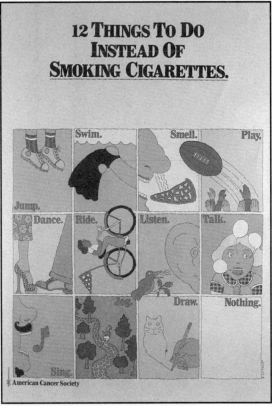

12 THINGS TO DO INSTEAD OF SMOKING CIGARETTES.

Swim. Smell. Play. Jump. Dance. Ride. Listen. Talk. Jog. Draw. Nothing. Sing.

American Cancer Society

Smoking tobacco is an addiction.

addiction

Have you ever felt a very strong desire to eat a candy bar? You wanted one so badly that you didn't think you could go without one. An addiction feels much worse. People who have an addiction must take a particular drug or other substance all the time or they will not feel good.

In the United States, illegal drugs include marijuana, cocaine, and heroin. People use these drugs to try to relax, or to feel more awake, or to forget their problems. They believe they can use a drug a few times and then stop. Many people become addicted, however, and cannot stop.

When people are becoming addicted, they start to use drugs more often. They turn away from friends and family. They begin to have trouble at school or at work. They spend most of their time thinking about their next dose of the drug. If they do not get it, they may feel dizzy, shaky, and sick to their stomachs. When they take the drug, they feel good again, but only for a short time. The effect of the drug wears off, and their bodies begin to crave another dose.

People may also become addicted to legal drugs. One of these is alcohol. It is found in drinks such as beer, wine, and whiskey. Many people use alcohol without becoming addicted. Others find that they need to drink more and more in order to feel happy and relaxed. Eventually, no matter how much they drink, they don't feel happy anymore. Drinking becomes a problem in their lives. Their work may suffer, and they make their families and friends unhappy.

Addiction to alcohol is called *alcoholism.* People with this addiction are *alcoholics.* Alcoholics depend on alcohol to feel good. But if they keep drinking, alcohol will ruin their health. Alcoholism is a serious disease that is hard to cure. Anyone who has a problem with alcohol should get help. Alcoholics Anonymous—AA—is an organization that helps alcoholics themselves. Al-Anon, a similar organization, helps their families.

Some drugs that doctors prescribe can also be addictive. If such drugs are used properly, they are helpful. But if they are abused, a person can become addicted.

Tobacco contains an addictive drug called *nicotine.* That is why people who smoke must keep on smoking in order to feel normal. Smokers are more likely to have high blood pressure and heart attacks. Many smokers develop lung diseases, such as bronchitis, emphysema, and lung cancer.

Treatment programs may help people break their addictions. Schools and special groups are helping people understand the dangers of drugs. For those who do not use addictive drugs, the best advice is—don't start!

See also **alcohol; drugs and medicines;** and **tobacco.**

addition, *see* arithmetic

adolescence, *see* growth, human

Adopted children become full members of their new families.

adoption

If a child is born to parents who are not able to take care of it, new parents may ask to adopt the child. By adoption, a child born to one set of parents becomes the legal child of other parents. The adopted child has the same rights as a child born into a family. The new parents agree to care for their adopted child in the same way they would care for a child born to them.

Most adoptions are arranged by adoption agencies. These agencies have lists of children who are available for adoption. The agencies also have lists of people who want to adopt children. The agency checks to be sure that a child is healthy, and that the people who want to adopt will be good parents. Then it gives the child to the new parents. Adoptions may also be arranged by a lawyer without an adoption agency.

Before an adoption is final, there is usually a trial period of 6 to 12 months. If all goes well, the new parents appear in court and officially adopt the child as their own.

Once a child has been adopted, the *natural parents*—the birth parents—give up all rights to the child as well as all responsibility for him or her. They cannot change their minds and ask to have the child back. They usually do not know the name of the child's new family, and the new family does not know the names of the natural parents.

As adopted children grow older, some want to find out who their natural parents are. This is often difficult because most adoption records are kept secret. Still, many adults who were adopted as children have found their natural parents.

In countries where there have been wars, there are many *orphans*—children whose parents have died. Some of these children have been adopted by families in the United States.

advertising

Advertising is a way of sending a message to a large number of people. An advertisement, also called an *ad,* usually tells people about a product they might want to buy, such as a kind of car, soap, or candy bar.

We see and hear hundreds of ads every week, in newspapers and magazines, on radio, television, and signs. We may see 400 to 500 ads every day! In fact, we see so many ads that we hardly notice most of them.

Advertising existed as far back as ancient Egypt. People who could not read could understand signs with pictures on them. Storeowners today still put up signs to let shoppers know what they sell. Giant billboards line many streets and highways. There are ads on buses and taxis.

More advertising is done in newspapers than anywhere else. People put small ads for things like used bicycles in the classified section of the paper. In other parts of the newspaper, supermarkets and other stores advertise their sales—special low prices on food, clothes, and other items. They hope people who see the ads will hurry in to buy the sale items.

Many big companies advertise in magazines. They also buy advertising time on radio and television stations. Radio and television ads are called *commercials.*

Other advertisers send messages by mail to people they hope will buy their products. Some send thick catalogs filled with pictures of all the things they sell.

Advertising is important to business. It helps sell a product by telling people about the product's good points. Sometimes, advertising may even help keep prices lower. For example, a company that advertises might sell millions of bicycles a year. That company could then make and sell more bicycles a year for less money than a company that sells only a few thousand a year.

Advertising is not always helpful. Some ads promise things that are not true, and some urge us to buy things we don't need. Many people think there is too much advertising. They want billboards taken down and do not want commercials that interrupt television shows.

Even people who don't like advertising might be surprised if it all suddenly stopped. Advertising gives us much useful information for everyday life.

Advertising is part of our lives. We may see hundreds of ads every day.

Aerobic exercise helps keep the heart and lungs healthy and strong.

aerobic exercise

What is one of the first things you notice about yourself when you exercise? You may find that you breathe faster and harder than you normally do. That's because your muscles need oxygen to work, and you get oxygen from the air you breathe.

Exercise also makes your heart pump faster. This is because blood pumped by the heart carries oxygen from your lungs to your muscles. The heart pumps faster to move more oxygen-filled blood to the muscles.

Exercise that makes your lungs and heart work hard to bring oxygen to your muscles is called *aerobic* (air-OH-bik) exercise. The word *aerobic* comes from two Greek words—*aeros,* meaning "air," and *bios,* meaning "life."

Not all exercise is aerobic. Some exercises, such as weight lifting and short running races, are called *anaerobic* exercises. They require short bursts of strength or speed. To do them, you do not need to breathe in extra oxygen. Instead, anaerobic exercises use up the oxygen already stored in the muscles.

Aerobic exercises keep you moving for 20 minutes or more without stopping. Some popular aerobic exercises are jogging, distance running, bicycling, skating, swimming, and walking. Aerobic dancing is offered at many health clubs.

When you exercise regularly, your lungs get better at taking oxygen from the air. Your heart gets better at pumping oxygen-filled blood to your muscles. Your muscles become better at using the oxygen. Soon, you are able to exercise harder and longer.

Aerobic exercise is healthful and fun. While you are running, bicycling, or dancing, you are building up your lungs and heart. This helps you avoid heart disease and some other illnesses. Regular aerobic exercise also helps you build muscles and stay slim.

If you haven't been exercising regularly, start slowly. If you start too quickly, you will be tired in only a few minutes. Remember that it is important to do any aerobic exercise for at least 20 minutes at a time.

aerospace, *see* astronaut; satellite; space exploration

Aesop, *see* fable

Afghanistan

Capital: Kabul	
Area: 250,000 square miles (647,500 square kilometers)	
Population (1985): about 15,056,000	
Official languages: Pushtu, Dari	

Afghanistan is a rugged, mountainous country in southwest Asia. It is almost as big as Texas but has no outlet to the sea. The country borders Iran to the west, the Soviet Union to the north, and Pakistan to the east and south. In the far northwest, a narrow strip of

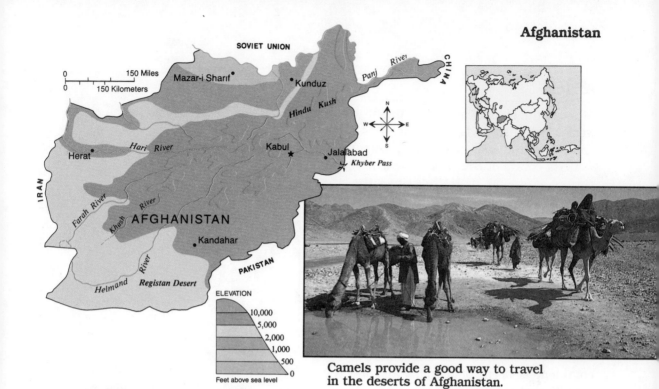

ELEVATION

10,000
5,000
2,000
1,000
500
0

Feet above sea level

Camels provide a good way to travel
in the deserts of Afghanistan.

land sticks out like a finger to touch China.

Long ago, Afghanistan was known as the "Forbidden Kingdom." People from other countries were not welcome there. Even today, few people travel to Afghanistan. There are few ways to travel around the country, and Afghanistan is very poor. For many years, a violent civil war has kept visitors out of the country.

Much of Afghanistan is covered by steep mountains. Peaks in the Hindu Kush range reach 25,000 feet (7,620 meters). The highest mountains run along Afghanistan's southeastern border with Pakistan. In northern and southwestern Afghanistan, there are dry hills and plains.

Nearly three out of every four Afghans are farmers or herders. Farmers grow fruits, nuts, and cotton in the lowlands. High in the mountains, herders raise sheep for wool. Some of the wool is used to make colorful rugs and carpets.

Most Afghans are Muslims—followers of the Islamic religion. Many different peoples live in the country. The largest group, the Pushtuns, live mostly in the valleys of the Hindu Kush. The second-largest group, the Tajiks, live in the dry hills and plains of the North and Southwest.

Kabul, Afghanistan's capital and largest city, is in a valley of the Hindu Kush mountains. To the east of Kabul is the Khyber Pass, a natural gap in the mountains. The pass connects Afghanistan and Pakistan. It has been a route for traders and conquerors throughout history. Alexander the Great and his army used the Khyber Pass to cross the Hindu Kush mountains in 330 B.C.

Many ancient peoples traveled through present-day Afghanistan and conquered parts of it. In the 1700s, the Afghan tribes united. Afghanistan became an independent country. During the 1800s, Russia and Britain wanted to control the new country. Britain gained control in 1879 and kept power until 1919, when Afghanistan became independent again.

In the late 1970s, a civil war broke out. Communist leaders revolted against the noncommunist government. The revolt succeeded, and in 1978 the Soviet Union sent soldiers into Afghanistan to help the new communist government. But fighting continued. Many Afghans were killed in the war, and many more left their country. Most went to neighboring Pakistan.

Africa

Africa is the second-largest continent in the world. Only Asia is larger. Africa has huge deserts, wild jungles, and vast grasslands.

Africa covers one-fifth of the earth's land surface. It is more than three times the size of the United States. It is about 5,000 miles (8,100 kilometers) long from north to south. At its widest point, it is more than 4,500 miles (7,300 kilometers) from east to west.

Africa lies south of Europe and the Middle East. Its northern coast is on the Mediterranean Sea. The Atlantic Ocean lies to the west, and the Indian Ocean is to the east.

The equator passes through Africa just south of its middle. The larger part of the continent is north of the equator, and the smaller part is south of it.

Over 500 million people live in Africa —more than twice the number of people in the United States. About three-fourths of all Africans are black. There are also many Arabs, as well as some Europeans, Asians, and people of mixed ancestry.

Africa is a troubled continent. Its people are among the poorest in the world. Many cannot read or write. Thousands die of starvation each year.

Yet Africa is also a continent of hope. Most of Africa used to be controlled by nations in Europe. In the 1950s, however, Africans began to win their independence and started to build new countries. Almost all of the 51 African countries are less than 50 years old.

Africa may be thought of as divided into two huge areas with very different lands and peoples. North Africa includes the Sahara Desert and runs north to the Mediterranean Sea. The region to the south of the Sahara is sub-Saharan Africa.

North Africa The Sahara—the world's largest desert—takes up more than one-fourth of the area of Africa. (*See* **Sahara.**)

Between the Sahara and the shore of the Mediterranean Sea lies a coastal region where rain falls and food crops grow. Many people live along this fertile strip of land, in

Nairobi, the capital of Kenya, is a bustling modern city.

Morocco, Algeria, Tunisia, Libya, and Egypt. Large cities, like Alexandria, Algiers, and Cairo (which is Africa's largest city), dot the coastline. North African farmers grow wheat, barley, grapes, and other crops.

The Nile River is the longest river in the world. It starts near the equator in the Sudan and flows north through the Sudan and Egypt until it reaches the Mediterranean. Most Egyptians live in the Nile River Valley. They grow cotton, rice, sugarcane, and corn, using water from the river.

The peoples of North Africa are mostly Arabs. They speak Arabic, and they are Muslims—followers of the Islamic religion. The peoples of North Africa have close ties with Muslims in the Middle East.

The countries along the southern Sahara include Mauritania, Mali, Niger, Chad, and the Sudan. Arabs and other Muslims live in the northern parts of these countries. Blacks live in the southern parts. Muslims and blacks sometimes fight each other for control of the countries.

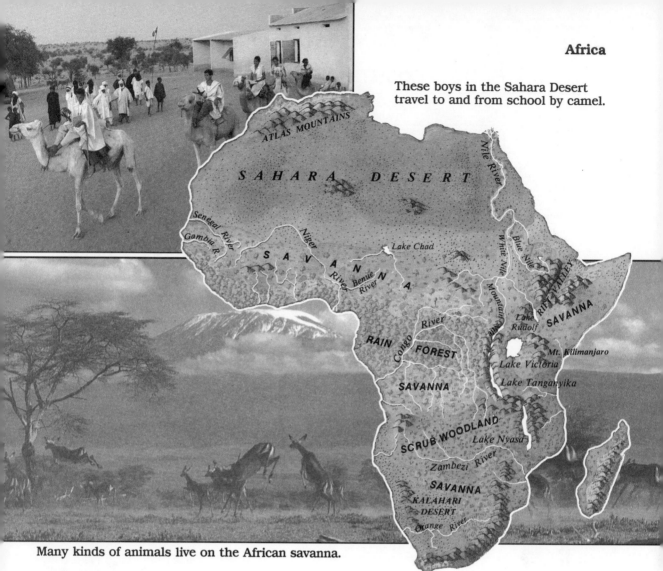

These boys in the Sahara Desert travel to and from school by camel.

Many kinds of animals live on the African savanna.

Sub-Saharan Africa The region south of the Sahara has many kinds of land: grasslands, rain forests, and deserts.

The highest mountain in Africa is Mount Kilimanjaro in Tanzania, a country in the eastern sub-Sahara. This region also has many large lakes. Lake Victoria is the second-largest freshwater lake in the world next to Lake Superior in North America.

In western sub-Saharan Africa, two great rivers flow into the Atlantic. The Niger flows along the edge of the Sahara and empties into the sea in Nigeria. Farther south, the Congo flows through dense rain forests near the equator.

The Zambezi River in southern Africa is the largest river flowing into the Indian Ocean. In Zimbabwe, the river flows over Victoria Falls, which is twice as high as Niagara Falls in North America.

Africa has long been known for its rain forests, sometimes called jungles. The African rain forests along the equator are among the wildest in the world. Few people live there, but the rain forests are full of chattering monkeys, thousands of colorful birds, and many other animals.

Most of sub-Saharan Africa is made up of grasslands and plains. The grasslands, which are called *savannas*, stretch for hundreds of miles. Elephants, giraffes, zebras, lions, and many other animals live in the savannas. The lion is not "king of the jungle," because he doesn't live there—but he may be "king of the savanna"!

Thousands of large African animals have been hunted and killed. Some may soon become extinct. Today, animals in Africa are protected in game parks, where they can be seen and photographed, but not hunted.

COUNTRIES OF AFRICA

Country	Capital	Square Miles	Square Kilometers	Population
Algeria	Algiers	919,591	2,381,739	22,107,000
Angola	Luanda	481,351	1,246,698	7,948,000
Benin	Porto-Novo	43,483	112,621	4,015,000
Botswana	Gaborone	231,804	600,372	1,068,000
Burkina Faso	Ouagadougou	105,869	274,200	6,907,000
Burundi	Bujumbura	10,747	27,835	4,673,000
Cameroon	Yaoundé	183,568	475,441	9,737,000
Cape Verde	Praia	1,557	4,033	312,000
Central African Republic	Bangui	240,534	622,983	2,664,000
Chad	N'Djamena	496,000	1,284,000	5,036,000
Comoros	Moroni	838	2,170	469,000
Congo	Brazzaville	132,000	342,000	1,798,000
Djibouti	Djibouti	8,500	22,000	297,000
Egypt	Cairo	386,660	1,001,449	49,133,000
Equatorial Guinea	Malabo	10,830	28,050	350,000
Ethiopa	Addis Ababa	471,800	1,221,900	42,266,000
Gabon	Libreville	103,346	267,666	988,000
Gambia	Banjul	4,361	11,295	751,000
Ghana	Accra	92,099	238,536	13,004,000
Guinea	Conakry	94,964	245,957	5,597,000
Guinea-Bissau	Bissau	13,948	36,125	858,000
Ivory Coast	Abidjan	124,503	322,463	10,090,000
Kenya	Nairobi	224,960	582,646	20,194,000
Lesotho	Maseru	11,720	30,355	1,512,000
Liberia	Monrovia	43,000	111,370	2,232,000
Libya	Tripoli	679,359	1,759,538	3,752,000
Madagascar	Antananarivo	226,657	587,041	9,941,000
Malawi	Lilongwe	45,747	118,485	7,056,000
Mali	Bamako	478,764	1,239,998	7,721,000
Mauritania	Nouakchott	397,954	1,030,700	1,656,000
Mauritius	Port Louis	790	2,046	1,011,000
Morocco	Rabat	172,413	446,549	23,117,000
Mozambique	Maputo	309,494	801,589	13,638,000
Namibia (South-West Africa)	Windhoek	318,259	824,290	1,108,000
Niger	Niamey	489,200	1,267,000	6,491,000
Nigeria	Lagos	356,667	923,767	102,783,000
Rwanda	Kigali	10,169	26,338	6,249,000
São Tomé and Príncipe	São Tomé	372	963	105,000
Senegal	Dakar	75,750	196,192	6,755,000
Seychelles	Victoria	171	444	66,000
Sierra Leone	Freetown	27,699	71,740	3,883,000
Somalia	Mogadishu	246,200	637,658	7,595,000
South Africa	Cape Town Pretoria	471,443	1,221,036	32,465,000
Sudan	Khartoum	967,495	2,505,810	22,972,000
Swaziland	Mbabane	6,704	17,363	671,000
Tanzania	Dar es Salaam	364,898	945,085	21,701,000
Togo	Lomé	21,622	56,001	3,023,000
Tunisia	Tunis	63,170	163,610	7,259,000
Uganda	Kampala	91,134	236,037	14,689,000
Western Sahara*	Aaiun	103,000	266,770	91,000
Zaire	Kinshasa	905,563	2,345,406	30,505,000
Zambia	Lusaka	290,584	752,612	6,832,000
Zimbabwe	Harare	150,803	390,579	8,678,000
TOTAL		11,710,114	30,328,551	565,819,000

*occupied by Morocco

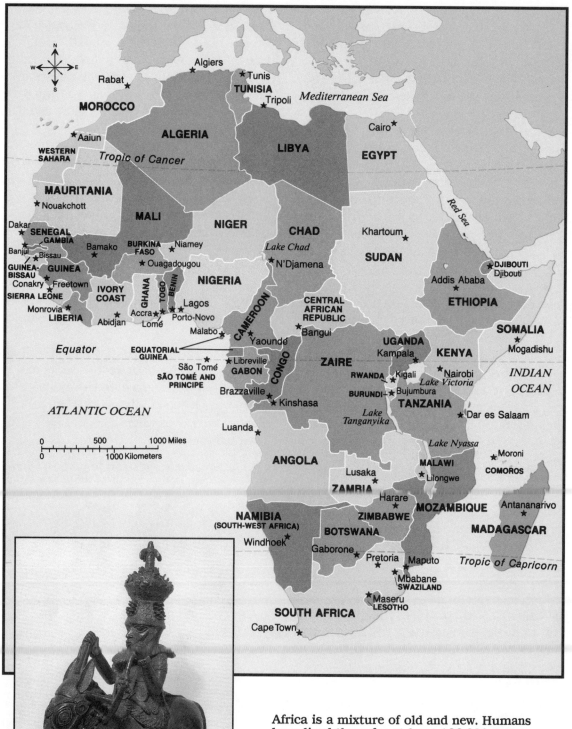

N
W—E
S

Algiers ★
Rabat ★   ★ Tunis
MOROCCO   **TUNISIA**   ★ Tripoli   *Mediterranean Sea*

Cairo ★

ALGERIA   **LIBYA**   **EGYPT**

★ Aaiun
WESTERN SAHARA   *Tropic of Cancer*

Red Sea

MAURITANIA
★ Nouakchott

Dakar   **MALI**   **NIGER**   **CHAD**   Khartoum ★
★ **SENEGAL**
★ **GAMBIA**   Bamako ★   **BURKINA FASO**   ★ Niamey   **SUDAN**
Banjul   ★ Bissau   ★ Ouagadougou   *Lake Chad*   ★ N'Djamena   ★ **DJIBOUTI**
GUINEA-BISSAU   **GUINEA**   **NIGERIA**   Djibouti
Conakry ★   ★ Freetown   **IVORY COAST**   Addis Ababa ★
SIERRA LEONE   **CENTRAL AFRICAN REPUBLIC**   **ETHIOPIA**
Monrovia ★   Accra ★   Lagos
LIBERIA   Abidjan ★   Lomé   Porto-Novo   Bangui ★   **SOMALIA**
Malabo ★   **CAMEROON**   Yaoundé ★   **UGANDA**   ★ Mogadishu
Equator   **EQUATORIAL GUINEA**   Kampala ★   **KENYA**
São Tomé ★   ★ Libreville   **CONGO**   **ZAIRE**   **RWANDA** ★ Kigali   ★ Nairobi   *INDIAN OCEAN*
SÃO TOMÉ AND PRINCIPE   **GABON**   Brazzaville ★   **BURUNDI** ★ Bujumbura   *Lake Victoria*
★ Kinshasa   **TANZANIA**   ★ Dar es Salaam
Lake Tanganyika

ATLANTIC OCEAN

0   500   1000 Miles
0   1000 Kilometers

Luanda ★   *Lake Nyassa*   ★ Moroni
MALAWI   **COMOROS**
ANGOLA   Lusaka ★   ★ Lilongwe
ZAMBIA   Antananarivo ★
Harare ★   **MOZAMBIQUE**
NAMIBIA (SOUTH-WEST AFRICA)   **ZIMBABWE**   **MADAGASCAR**
BOTSWANA   *Tropic of Capricorn*
Windhoek ★   Gaborone ★   Pretoria ★   ★ Maputo
Mbabane ★
SWAZILAND
★ Maseru **LESOTHO**
SOUTH AFRICA
Cape Town ★

Africa is a mixture of old and new. Humans have lived there for at least 100,000 years. But most of Africa's countries have been started in the last 50 years. The statue at left was made between 1400 and 1700 in western Africa.

People The people of Africa belong to hundreds of different tribes. For example, about 250 different tribes live in the large country of Nigeria, in the western sub-Sahara. For many Africans, their tribe is like a giant family that will take care of its members and protect them.

Since many tribes have their own languages, hundreds of different languages are spoken in Africa. This makes it difficult for even neighboring tribes to talk to each other. Many Africans speak a second language. In East Africa, Swahili is an important second language spoken by people in many tribes. In other parts of Africa, English or French is the second language.

Nearly three out of four Africans are herders or farmers. Most farmers have small plots of land and grow just enough food to feed themselves and their families. They farm with simple tools. Very few have tractors or other modern farm machinery.

There are a few farmers who grow *cash crops*—crops for sale. Cacao, the main ingredient of chocolate, is an important cash crop. Farmers also grow coffee, peanuts, cotton, and bananas for sale.

Some Africans live in cities, in homes or apartments like those in the United States. Many poor Africans from small villages come to the cities looking for work. Because there is little industry, they cannot always find jobs. Some go back to their villages. Others live in shantytowns at the edges of the cities.

Only a small number of Africans can read or write. Most children go to school for only two or three years, or not at all. African governments are working hard to build more schools and train more teachers.

History Humans have lived in Africa for at least 150,000 years, longer than anywhere else in the world.

Africa gave the world one of its first great civilizations. More than 5,000 years ago, the Egyptians built a powerful nation along the banks of the Nile River. Ancient Egypt ruled a great empire that reached deep into eastern Africa. (*See* **Egypt, ancient.**)

North Africa was later ruled by peoples from the Middle East and Europe. The Greeks built cities there, and the Romans made North Africa part of their empire. Then, beginning in the 600s, warriors from the Arabian peninsula conquered the area. They introduced the new religion Islam to North Africa.

While the Arabs were conquering the North, black kings were ruling farther south. The kingdoms of Ghana, Mali, and Songhai grew strong in the western sub-Sahara, then gradually disappeared. (*See* **African civilizations.**)

Beginning in the 1400s, Europeans began to explore the western coast of Africa. In the 1500s, they needed strong workers for their colonies in the Americas. They sent men to West Africa to capture black Africans as slaves.

Between 1500 and 1850, about 10 million Africans were brought to the Americas as slaves. They were forced to live and work on their owners' plantations. In the 1800s, most of the slaves were freed, but only a few returned to Africa.

This father teaches his son to play the drums in the African country called the Ivory Coast.

Meanwhile, the countries of Europe continued to explore Africa, looking for valuable minerals and crops. They took control of one African region after another, until they ruled most of the continent. Britain, France, Belgium, Germany, Portugal, Spain, and Italy all had their own colonies. In 1914, all but two of the countries in Africa were ruled by Europeans. Many Africans worked in the mines and plantations owned by Europeans.

Missionaries came from Europe and the United States, and millions of Africans became Christians. The Europeans built roads and railroads, so that different regions could trade with each other. Fewer and fewer Africans followed a traditional way of life.

These African women live in a small village, but they wear clothing much like ours.

Africans began to try to free themselves from the rule of Europeans. Some European countries fought wars against the Africans to keep their colonies. Others gave up their colonies peacefully. Between 1951 and 1980, all the colonies disappeared, and 47 new African nations grew up in their place. Once free, Africans adopted some European ideas about government and business.

Southern Africa followed a different path than the rest of the continent. In the 1800s, thousands of British and Dutch settlers came to southern Africa. They mined gold and diamonds and built farms and ranches. Their countries, Rhodesia and South Africa, became richer than any others in Africa.

Like the other African countries, Rhodesia and South Africa became independent nations. But in these two countries, the white settlers controlled the governments. They forced blacks to live apart from whites, and did not allow them to vote.

In the 1970s, the blacks demanded power. In 1979, they took over the government of Rhodesia and changed the country's name to Zimbabwe. In South Africa, whites kept control, but there were many violent battles between blacks and white settlers. (*See* **South Africa**.)

These Africans are at an important meeting of business people from around the world.

Africa Today   The young countries of Africa face many problems. Their greatest problem is hunger. Africa is very beautiful, but much of the land is not good for farming. Long periods without rain have caused millions to die of starvation.

Other problems are caused by the differences among the many peoples of Africa. Many Africans are more loyal to their tribes than they are to their country. In some nations, civil wars have been fought between different tribes.

African countries are trying to solve their problems. They want to improve farming to grow more food. They want to build factories that will give people work. They need more new roads and airports so that their people can trade with each other. They also need more schools to train people to improve life in their countries.

These improvements will take time and a great deal of money. African nations are working together on their problems. They are also getting help from the richer nations of the world, including the United States.

See also **Algeria; Egypt; Ethiopia; Ghana; Kenya; Libya; Morocco; Nigeria; South Africa; Sudan; Zaire;** and **Zambia.**

African civilizations

Early peoples had a simple way of life. They hunted or farmed to survive. Some groups of people developed a more complicated way of life. Their societies are called *civilizations.* Civilized people build towns and cities, trade with other peoples, and create fine arts and crafts. Africa was the home of some great ancient civilizations.

On a map, you can see that much of Africa lies south of the Sahara Desert. This huge desert is so dry and hot that few people live or travel there even today. The Sahara forms a barrier that separates North Africa from sub-Saharan Africa, which is the part south of the Sahara.

North Africa is the portion of the continent that lies along the shore of the Mediterra-

nean Sea. Egypt, which has one of the oldest civilizations in the world, is located in this part of Africa. (*See* **Egypt, ancient.**)

North Africa is close to Europe and western Asia. People from those continents built many settlements in North Africa. The Phoenicians, the Greeks, the Romans, the Arabs, and the Turks all had cities there.

The civilizations of sub-Saharan Africa were very different from those in North Africa. Most of the peoples of North Africa are white. Most of those in sub-Saharan Africa are black. The ancestors of black Americans came from sub-Saharan Africa.

Until about 100 years ago, Europeans and Americans knew almost nothing about this southern part of the continent. Since then, we have learned much about its peoples and civilizations. Most of the peoples of sub-Saharan Africa did not have ways of writing

This ancient crown of the Ethiopian emperors was first worn by the rulers of Axum before A.D. 400.

This mosque—a temple of the Islamic religion—was built in the desert city of Timbuktu in the 1300s. Timbuktu was then part of the great Mali empire.

things down, so they left few written records. But anthropologists have studied the remains of buildings and other things the peoples left behind. We have also learned things from African stories and legends, and from the writings of foreign visitors.

Eastern Africa The first civilizations of sub-Saharan Africa were in the eastern part of the continent, south of Egypt. One kingdom was called Kush. It began about 3,000 years ago. The Kushites were known for the iron they mined, and for the iron hoes and spears they made. The people of Kush traded these to the Egyptians and to merchants who came by boat from the Near East, across the Red Sea or the Arabian Sea.

The most important city in Kush was Meroe. Here the Kushite civilization reached its height, between 250 B.C. and A.D. 150. The people of Meroe built steep pyramids as tombs for their kings, as the Egyptians had done thousands of years earlier. The Kushites also developed a kind of writing, but today no one can understand it.

Warriors from farther south conquered Kush and destroyed Meroe sometime in the 300s. These fighters came from another East African kingdom, Axum. The people of Axum were traders, too. Their merchants handled many different kinds of goods—

gold, silver, slaves, and the ivory from elephant tusks. Ruins found in this region show that the Axumites were very good builders. They could construct sturdy walls without using any mortar to hold the stones together. The Axumites are also known for farming on *terraces*—fields built into the sides of hills like huge shelves.

Sometime around A.D. 350, a missionary traveled to Axum from the North. He converted the king, Ezana, to Christianity. The descendants of the Axumites live in Ethiopia today. Many are still Christians.

Western Africa Far to the west, three great African kingdoms rose and fell, one after the other. The first was Ghana, which lay north of the country now called by the same name. The kingdom of Ghana was most important in the 900s. Its kings taxed the people in order to pay for an army of 200,000 men. Traders from Ghana traveled south to obtain gold from other African peoples. Then they used it to buy goods, especially salt, from North Africans who traveled across the Sahara in camel caravans.

In time, Ghana lost its power and was taken over by another, larger empire known as Mali. The modern nation of Mali is named after the ancient empire, but its borders are not quite the same. Mali was strongest in the

1300s. By this time, North Africa had been conquered by Arabs. Most North Africans were Muslims—followers of the Islamic religion. The merchants who crossed the Sahara to Mali from North Africa carried the ideas of this religion along with their trade goods. Many West Africans became Muslims.

Can you imagine going on a trip thousands of miles long with 60,000 people? Mali's greatest king, Mansa Musa, did this around the year 1325. He made a *pilgrimage* —a religious journey—to the Muslim holy city of Mecca in Arabia. Every night servants set up tents, and cooks made a meal for the travelers. Mansa Musa brought gold, to buy supplies along the way. He had 80 camels, and each of them carried 300 pounds (135 kilograms) of gold.

Like Ghana, Mali lost its power. In its place rose a third great empire, called Songhai. It ruled a large area of West Africa in the 1400s and 1500s. Under this empire, the city of Timbuktu became known for its Muslim university, Sankore. People came from all over to study there. A traveler to Timbuktu in the 1500s wrote that its people were "of a gentle and cheerful disposition."

Southern Africa In southeast Africa, there are many ruins of ancient stone buildings called *zimbabwes*. These were built by the Karanga people over 500 years ago in the country that is now called Zimbabwe. The Karangas mined gold. People exploring this region have found over 7,000 mine shafts dug into the ground.

The Karangas must have been wealthy, because they built very large structures. A fortress called Great Zimbabwe was their capital. Here the Karangas constructed buildings with walls 30 feet (9 meters) high and 20 feet (6 meters) thick. One, called the Temple, has a huge circular wall 800 feet (240 meters) around. This probably protected the houses where the king, his family, and their servants lived.

In time, Great Zimbabwe was deserted and fell into ruins. We may never know why all of its people left. This is only one

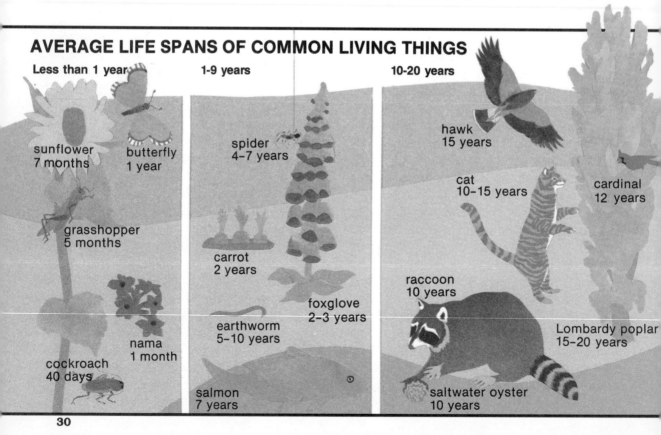

AVERAGE LIFE SPANS OF COMMON LIVING THINGS

Less than 1 year

sunflower
7 months

butterfly
1 year

grasshopper
5 months

nama
1 month

cockroach
40 days

1-9 years

spider
4–7 years

carrot
2 years

foxglove
2–3 years

earthworm
5–10 years

salmon
7 years

10-20 years

hawk
15 years

cat
10–15 years

cardinal
12 years

raccoon
10 years

Lombardy poplar
15–20 years

saltwater oyster
10 years

of the many mysteries about African civilizations of the past.

From Past to Present Since most African peoples did not have writing, they passed information from parents to children in stories and chants. Today, Africans still preserve some of their history and traditions in songs and stories. Some stories from western Africa were carried to America by slaves. Even when the slaves were forced to stop speaking their own languages, they remembered the stories, and some are told to this day.

See also **Africa.**

age

Age is the length of time that something has existed. If you are in third grade, your age is about 8 years. This means you were born 8 years ago. You are quite young for a human being. You can expect to live 70 to 80 years. Another way to say this is that a human being's life span is about 75 years.

On the other hand, a dog that is 8 years old is not young, because the life span of a dog is about 12 years. To compare dogs' ages to people's ages, we sometimes estimate that one year in a dog's life equals about seven years in a human's life. A dog that is 8 years old is about as far through its life as a person who is 56 years old.

Some living things have very short life spans. Some bacteria live for 20 minutes and then divide to make two new bacteria. A mayfly lives for a year underwater as a larva, then lives only one day as an adult. Many plants live for one growing season, from spring until frost.

Other living things have very long life spans. Giant sequoia trees can live 2,500 years. The bristlecone pine is the oldest known tree. Some bristlecone pines are more than 3,000 years old!

See also **life cycle.**

agriculture, *see* farming

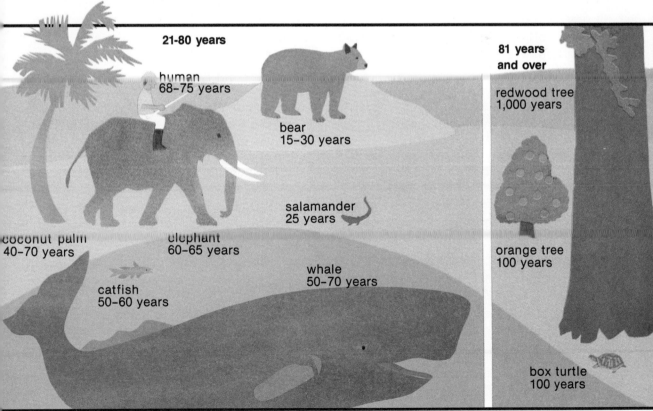

21-80 years

human
68–75 years

bear
15–30 years

coconut palm
40–70 years

elephant
60–65 years

salamander
25 years

catfish
50–60 years

whale
50–70 years

**81 years
and over**

redwood tree
1,000 years

orange tree
100 years

box turtle
100 years

Ailey, Alvin

Alvin Ailey is an American *choreographer* —a person who makes up dances. Ailey directs his own dance company and is known throughout the world for his exciting dances. Many of them are set to black folk music and jazz.

Alvin Ailey was born in Texas in 1931. He grew up in Los Angeles, California, where he learned to dance. In 1953, Ailey joined Lester Horton's dance company. When Horton died, Ailey began to make up dances for the group. His dances were a modern kind of ballet.

Ailey went to New York and performed in musical plays on Broadway. Soon, he formed his own group of dancers, called the Alvin Ailey American Dance Theater. At first, the group had only seven dancers, but it quickly grew and became successful.

The Alvin Ailey American Dance Theater has performed all over America and in 44 other countries. It was the first modern-dance group to perform in Russia. In 1984, it became the first black modern-dance company to play at New York's Metropolitan Opera House.

The Alvin Ailey American Dance Theater performs one of his modern dances.

Alvin Ailey has choreographed dances for many other ballet companies as well as for his own group. Because of his wide popularity, many young people from Africa, Asia, and Europe have come to the United States to become dancers.

See also **dance.**

air

Air is all around you. Though you cannot see it, taste it, or smell it, you can show that it exists. Push an upside-down glass straight down into a pan of water. Watch what happens. Because the "empty" glass is filled with air, water cannot enter. You also can feel the air. Moving air is the wind.

Air is a mixture of gases. About four-fifths of it is nitrogen. About one-fifth is oxygen. Air also contains small amounts of carbon dioxide, water vapor, and other gases. In addition, bits of dust are carried by the air. Dust comes from soil, smoke, car exhaust, and other sources.

Air is important to life. You can live for weeks without food. You can live for days without water. But you can live only a few minutes without air. Almost all living things need air to stay alive.

Plants and animals use the air in different ways. In sunlight, green plants combine carbon dioxide from the air with water from the soil to help make food. They send oxygen into the air. Animals take oxygen out of the air to help them make energy from their food. They put carbon dioxide back into the air. Some bacteria use nitrogen from the air.

See also **atmosphere; carbon dioxide; nitrogen;** and **oxygen.**

air conditioning

People have had many ways of keeping a room warm in the winter. Until the mid-1900s, however, they had very few ways of keeping a room cool in the summer. They opened windows and hoped for a breeze, or they closed windows to keep out the heat.

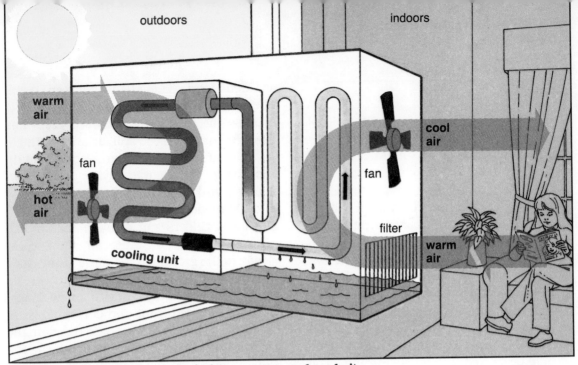

outdoors   indoors

warm air

hot air

fan

cooling unit

cool air

fan

filter

warm air

The air conditioner takes hot air from a room and cools it.
The warm air blows around coils filled with an ice-cold fluid.
The fluid soon becomes warmer. Pipes carry it to the cooling unit,
where it is cooled again. Outside air carries some of the heat away.

Throughout the year, rooms in homes and workplaces were often uncomfortable. They were either too hot, too cold, too stuffy, too dry, or too moist. Today, air conditioning can keep even a large building comfortable in any weather.

The air-conditioning system for a large building may fill a huge room. It can cool the air or heat it. Air conditioners used for a room or for an automobile are much smaller and can't be used for heating. In the summer, they blow cool, dry air through the room or the car.

Most air conditioners "condition" the hot summer air in the same ways. First, a fan sucks air into the air conditioner. The air passes through filters that remove most of the dust. An air-conditioned room is easier to keep clean than a room that is not.

Next, the air passes over coils of pipe that are filled with a very cold liquid. This cools the air, but at the same time, the heat from the air warms the liquid. As the liquid warms up, a pump pushes it to a refrigeration unit. This unit cools the liquid again. Then the liquid is pumped back into the cooling coils.

Cool air cannot hold as much water vapor as warm air. Therefore, as air cools in the air conditioner, some of the air's water vapor turns to liquid water and drains off. An air-conditioned room is comfortable partly because the air is drier—less humid.

When the air has been cleaned, cooled, and dried, a fan in the air conditioner blows it into the room and keeps it moving. This also helps keep people comfortable.

Large air conditioners used in big buildings also clean the air, cool it, and make it drier. In winter, however, these big air conditioners can also warm the air. Hot liquid in their coils of pipe warms the air.

Air conditioners pump "conditioned" air into all the rooms of a building through large pipes, called *air ducts.* Giant fans push the air through the ducts and keep it moving inside the rooms. After the air has circulated in a room, it is sucked into another duct and carried back to the air-conditioning unit. There it is cleaned and cooled or heated all over again. No matter how hot or cold it is outside, the air-conditioning system keeps the indoor weather pleasant all year.

See also **refrigeration.**

aircraft

Aircraft are machines that can fly. People have always wanted to fly. In ancient times, they built wings from wax and feathers and tried to fly like birds. They did not succeed.

Early Flight In 1783, people found one way to stay up in the air. They used balloons filled with hot air to float above the ground. But people could not control the balloons. The wind carried them wherever it was blowing. Often, this was not where the pilot of the balloon wanted to go. By the early 1900s, the problem was solved. Large balloons called *airships* were developed. These airships—blimps, zeppelins, and dirigibles —could be steered with an engine and a rudder. (*See* **balloon**.)

While some people were trying balloons, others were playing with kites. A simple kite works like the wing of a bird or an airplane. It catches the wind. As long as you keep the kite at the correct angle, the wind will keep it up in the air. The kite's string and perhaps a tail control the angle.

A kite stays up because the force of the wind builds up under the kite. Air pushing up from underneath pushes the kite higher. Air rushing over the top also helps to suck the kite up. This is because moving air has less pressure than air that is still. Try this experiment. Hold two strips of paper about an inch apart. Then blow between them. They will move toward each other. That is because the moving air between them has less pressure than the still air around them.

The total force of air that keeps a kite up is called *lift*. Sir George Cayley, an Englishman, studied lift in kites. In 1804, he began to build model gliders whose wings worked like kites. Gliders sail through the air like paper airplanes. In quiet air, they coast slowly to the ground. If the air is rising, they can soar higher and higher.

Cayley designed a wing with a new shape. It had a rounded front and curved down at the back. When the wing cut through the air, the underside caught the wind. At the same time, air flowed more quickly over the top. The push of air under the wing and the pull of lowered pressure above the wing gave more lift to Cayley's gliders.

During the 1800s, inventors worked on building a glider large enough to carry a person. By 1895, Otto Lilienthal, a German, was flying in his own large gliders. Some of his gliders had two sets of wings for greater lift.

The First Airplanes Gliders still had to go where the wind took them. If a glider had

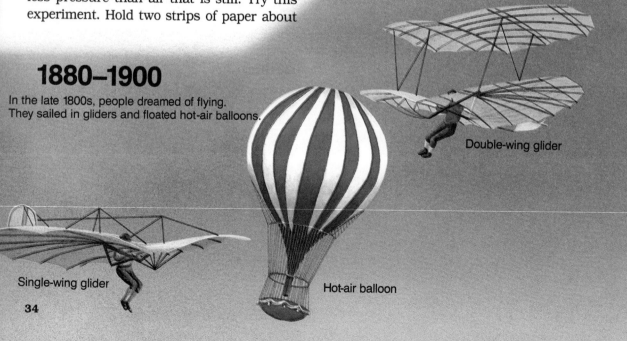

1880–1900

In the late 1800s, people dreamed of flying. They sailed in gliders and floated hot-air balloons.

Double-wing glider

Single-wing glider

Hot-air balloon

a light, powerful engine, a pilot could make it go wherever he or she wanted. A glider plus an engine equals an airplane.

The first airplanes were small models. One early model was built in 1848. It was powered by a lightweight steam engine that turned two propellers. It flew well, but it was too small for anyone to ride in.

On December 17, 1903, Americans Wilbur and Orville Wright attached a 12-horsepower gasoline engine to a glider they had built. On the first flight, Orville flew the plane for 12 seconds and traveled only 120 feet. Later that day, Wilbur set a new record. He stayed in the air for 59 seconds. Soon, the Wright brothers were flying longer flights with more powerful engines.

The Wright brothers' airplane had two propellers behind the main wings. The propellers pulled air in, over the wings. There were two smaller wings in front of the large main pair of wings. These smaller ones could be tilted to make the airplane go up or down. The pilot had to lie facedown on the bottom of the airplane. He steered by pulling wires attached to two rudders at the tail.

Builders of gliders and airplanes kept experimenting with the number of wings. The Wright brothers made their first flight in a biplane, which is a plane that has two sets of wings. A few triplanes, which have three sets of wings, were used in World War I (1914 to 1918). By 1909, there were also monoplanes—planes with only one set of wings. That year, Louis Blériot, a Frenchman, used a monoplane to cross the English Channel.

By the end of the 1920s, most new planes were monoplanes. Charles Lindbergh flew from New York to Paris in 1927 in a monoplane named *The Spirit of St. Louis*. He was the first person to fly alone across the Atlantic Ocean. His achievement helped make monoplanes popular.

Controlling the Airplane Wings are very important in controlling a plane. Movable flaps called *ailerons* are on the tips of the main wings. When one set of ailerons is raised, the set on the other wing is lowered. This causes the plane to tip left or right. Just as you lean your bicycle inward when you make a turn, a plane must lean to one side. This is called *banking*.

At the same time, the *rudder*—a flap on the tail—is turned. The rudder helps steer the plane the way a boat rudder steers a boat. Together, the ailerons and the rudder steer the plane to the left or right.

Elevators, which are other flaps on the tail, steer the plane up or down. Modern air-

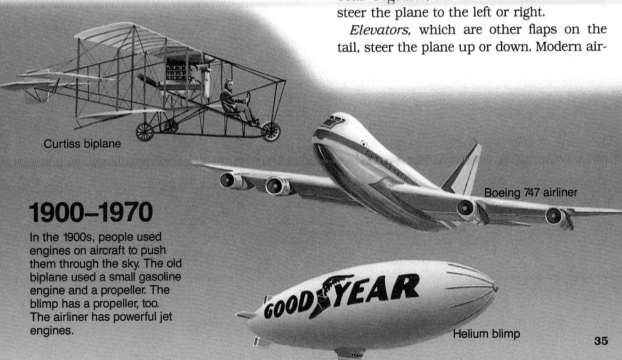

Curtiss biplane

Boeing 747 airliner

1900–1970

In the 1900s, people used engines on aircraft to push them through the sky. The old biplane used a small gasoline engine and a propeller. The blimp has a propeller, too. The airliner has powerful jet engines.

GOODYEAR

Helium blimp

35

planes have two elevators at the tail. They move up and down. The pilot uses the elevators to make the airplane climb or dive.

By 1912, pilots could operate the ailerons and elevators with one joystick. Pulling the joystick back made the plane climb. Pushing it forward made the plane dive toward the ground. Moving the joystick left or right made the plane bank to the left or right. You may have used a joystick for video games.

The rudder was controlled by a rudder bar, which had two pedals that the pilot pushed with his feet to turn the rudder right or left.

Propellers and Jets The Wright brothers' first successful airplane had only a 12-horsepower engine. Its two wooden propellers were located behind the wings.

There were many different propeller designs. Soon, most propellers were made of metal instead of wood. Some propellers had as many as six blades.

In 1927, the first three-engine airplanes were built. Each propeller had its own powerful engine. By World War II, large cargo planes and heavy bombers had four motors. Jet engines were first used on fighter planes.

In 1958, the Boeing 707 began flying passengers. Today, the Concorde passenger jet can reach a speed of 2,250 kilometers (1,400 miles) per hour. (*See* **jet engine.**)

Navigation The first pilots flew short distances at low altitudes. With the help of a compass and a map, pilots could look down to see where they were going. If it was cloudy or foggy, pilots could not fly safely.

Modern aircraft have radar as well as radio. The radar helps them "see" even in thick clouds at night. Pilots also receive radio signals that tell them if they are on course. Air traffic controllers on the ground keep track of all planes in their areas and can talk to the pilots by radio.

Before taking off, a pilot must give officials a flight plan. This tells where the plane is going and when it should arrive. No airplane can leave the ground until air traffic controllers clear it for takeoff.

Other Aircraft Four years after the Wright brothers' success, people began working to develop the helicopter. Early efforts failed because engines were not powerful enough. In the late 1930s, however,

The cockpit of a modern jet airplane has many gauges and instruments. The pilot and copilot must check them all before takeoff.

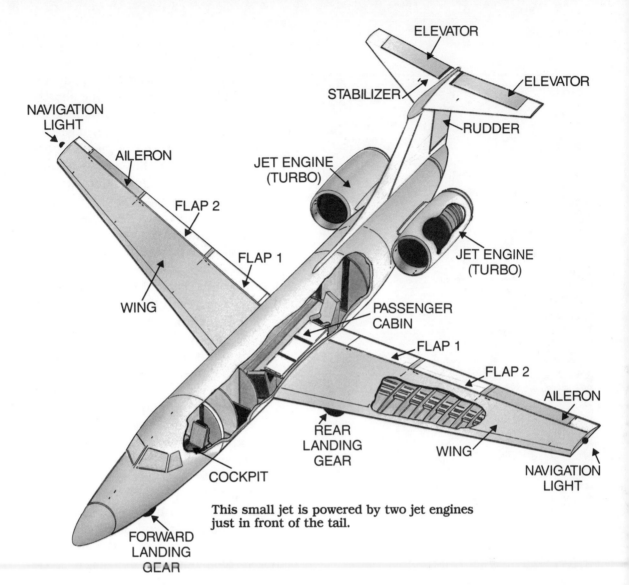

NAVIGATION LIGHT

AILERON

FLAP 2

FLAP 1

WING

ELEVATOR

ELEVATOR

STABILIZER

RUDDER

JET ENGINE (TURBO)

JET ENGINE (TURBO)

PASSENGER CABIN

FLAP 1

FLAP 2

AILERON

WING

NAVIGATION LIGHT

REAR LANDING GEAR

COCKPIT

FORWARD LANDING GEAR

This small jet is powered by two jet engines just in front of the tail.

Germany and the United States produced helicopters that flew well and could be controlled easily. (*See* **helicopter.**)

From 1947 through 1962, people experimented with planes powered by rockets. These flew faster and higher than any other aircraft, but were not suitable for passenger travel. They did contribute to the development of rocket-powered spacecraft. (*See* **rocket** and **space exploration.**)

Seaplanes can land and take off on water. Vertical-takeoff-and-landing aircraft (VTOLs) can take off by rising straight up, like a helicopter, and then fly like an airplane. Today's Harrier VTOL has jet engines with nozzles that can be turned in different directions.

Modern Aircraft The first pilots flew aircraft just for the thrill of it. Today, most aircraft do hard work. They carry passengers, mail, and other cargo. Some are used for taking pictures of the earth. Farmers use small planes to dust crops with insecticide. Foresters use them to drop chemicals on forest fires. Some aircraft are also powerful weapons. (*See* **fighter plane.**)

Modern aircraft can fly faster, higher, and longer than any bird. Today's jets have instruments, gauges, and controls that would amaze the Wright brothers. With all this technology, however, it is still not possible to build an airplane that can fly as easily and as gracefully as a bird.

See also **airport.**

air force, *see* **armed services**

Smog is created when sunlight reacts with car exhaust and other gases.

air pollution

Almost all plants and animals need air to live. When the air contains harmful substances, we say that it is *polluted.*

We can see some kinds of air pollution. The brown or yellow haze over a city, called *smog,* is air pollution caused mainly by fuel burning in the engines of thousands of cars and trucks. Smog irritates people's eyes and makes it hard to breathe. It also harms plants and animals. Smog has killed many palm trees and other plants along highways in southern California.

Other kinds of air pollution cannot be seen or felt but can still harm living things. Lichens are plants that need clean air. When they begin dying, it can mean that air pollution is becoming a serious problem, even if we don't notice the pollution itself.

Natural events can cause air pollution. For example, when a volcano erupts, it spits tons of gas and bits of material into the air. Termites add large amounts of carbon dioxide and other gases to the air as they digest the cell walls of plants. Termites may be small, but scientists estimate that all the termites on Earth together weigh about twice as much as all humans together.

Yet human activity causes most of the world's air pollution. In large cities, gases and soot from automobile, bus, and truck engines create very bad air pollution. Smoke and fumes that come from factories, the burning of trash, and the burning of oil for heat all make the problem worse.

Air pollution can also cause a kind of water pollution called *acid rain.* Sulfur and nitrogen compounds mix with moisture in the air and fall to Earth in rain or snow. Then this acid water runs into rivers and lakes. Many lakes in the northeastern United States and southeastern Canada are now so acid that fish cannot live in them. Acid rain also harms trees and other plants.

The United States and other countries have passed laws to help reduce air pollution. Cars and trucks and buses must have special equipment to reduce the amount of pollution they put into the air. Factories must clean dangerous materials from the smoke coming out of their chimneys. In many places, burning trash is not allowed, and homes and factories must burn fuels that produce less pollution.

See also **conservation** and **water pollution.**

airport

When you want to travel across the country by airplane, you start and end your trip in an airport. An airport is a place where airplanes take off and land.

There are several kinds of airports. People who fly their own planes use private airports. Many private airports are small. People who want to travel as passengers on regular flights use commercial airports.

There they can buy tickets to travel on regularly scheduled passenger flights. Some commercial airports are almost like cities. They have drugstores, restaurants, barbershops, and bookstores.

A large airport takes up a lot of space, usually near the edge of a city. *Runways,* strips of concrete on which planes take off and land, must be thousands of feet long. Giant buildings called *hangars* are like garages for airplanes, where planes are stored and repaired. Airports also need parking space for thousands of cars.

Some airports are so large that they have their own bus lines or train systems to move travelers from one part of the airport to another. They also have many vehicles to carry fuel and food to the planes and to load and unload baggage.

At any moment, dozens of aircraft may be getting ready to take off or land at a large airport. Those waiting to land are flying overhead at different speeds, at different altitudes, and in different directions. Those waiting to take off are in line at the end of the takeoff runway.

Air traffic controllers are in charge of the air traffic. They sit in a tower where they can see most of the airport. Radar helps them keep track of planes that are in the air, even at night or in bad weather. Pilots get their instructions from the controllers by radio. The pilots must wait for clearance—permission—from the tower before they may take off or land.

A few times each year, an airplane is hijacked somewhere in the world. A person with a gun or a bomb forces the pilot to fly the plane to a different airport. To protect against hijackers, airline passengers and baggage are examined by X-ray machines before going on an airplane. The X rays can find a gun, a knife, or a bomb.

The five busiest airports in the world are all in the United States. They are in Chicago, Atlanta, New York, Los Angeles, and Dallas–Fort Worth. O'Hare International Airport, in Chicago, serves more than 100,000 passengers on an average day.

See also **aircraft.**

---

air pressure, *see* **barometer**

---

airship, *see* **aircraft; balloon**

An airport is planned so that passengers and baggage can move smoothly to and from the planes.

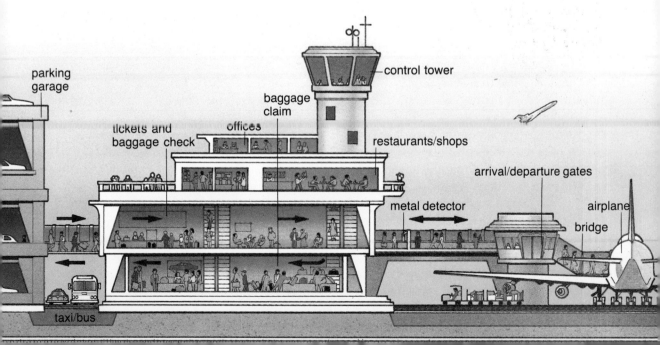

parking garage

baggage claim

tickets and baggage check

offices

control tower

restaurants/shops

arrival/departure gates

metal detector

airplane

bridge

taxi/bus

Alabama

Capital: Montgomery
Area: 51,705 square miles (133,916 square kilometers) (29th-largest state)
Population (1980): 3,890,061 (1985): about 4,021,000 (22nd-largest state)
Became a state: December 14, 1819 (22nd state)

Alabama is called the "Heart of Dixie." Dixie is a popular name for the southern United States. Alabama is located in the middle of the southern states and has played an important part in their history.

The Land The Appalachian Mountains reach into northeastern Alabama. Forests in the northern part of the state provide timber. The Tennessee River runs through the region. Huge dams on the river have power plants that provide electricity.

In south and central Alabama, there are rolling plains and fertile farmlands. The best farmland is in the Black Belt. It runs through the middle of the state and has rich, black soil. Soybeans and peanuts are the most important crops. Southwestern Alabama has a short coastline on the Gulf of Mexico. Mobile Bay is an important harbor.

People About half of Alabama's people live in or around cities. The others live in small towns or on farms. Alabama's largest city, Birmingham, is near the center of the state. Birmingham has many factories. They produce iron and steel and other products. Some of the coal used in making steel comes from mines in northern Alabama.

Mobile, the state's second-largest city, is a seaport on Mobile Bay. Huntsville, in the northern part of the state, is the home of the George C. Marshall Space Flight Center. The rockets that helped U.S. astronauts go to the moon were designed there. Huntsville is

sometimes called "Rocket City, U.S.A." Montgomery, the capital of Alabama, is near the center of the state.

About a quarter of the people of Alabama are black. Many are the descendants of slaves who worked on plantations and farms in Alabama.

History When Spanish explorers visited the region in the 1500s, they met Indian tribes. The area was later named after one of the tribes—the Alibamu.

In the 1700s, France claimed the land. Later, Britain and Spain claimed parts of it. Most of Alabama became part of the United States in 1783, after the American Revolution. In 1819, Alabama became the 22nd state.

Alabama came to be known as the Cotton State, because cotton was its most important crop. Growing cotton was hard work, however. The owners of cotton plantations had black slaves to do the work. Life for the slaves was hard and bitter.

In the 1850s, people in the northern states wanted to end slavery. Alabama and other southern states decided to leave the United States and form their own country—the Confederate States of America. Montgomery was the first capital of the new country.

Soon, the Civil War began. Thousands of soldiers from Alabama fought and died for the South. Cities and towns in northern and central Alabama were damaged. Plantations were burned.

After the war, Alabama joined the United States again. Slavery had ended, but many people—white and black—were poor and could not find work. They began making new products to sell, such as iron and steel, lumber and cloth.

Life was still hard for black people in Alabama. Even though they were free, state laws kept them out of good schools and made it hard for them to get jobs.

During the 1950s and 1960s, the black people of the state demanded their rights to go to school and work with white people. Martin Luther King, Jr., led demonstrations

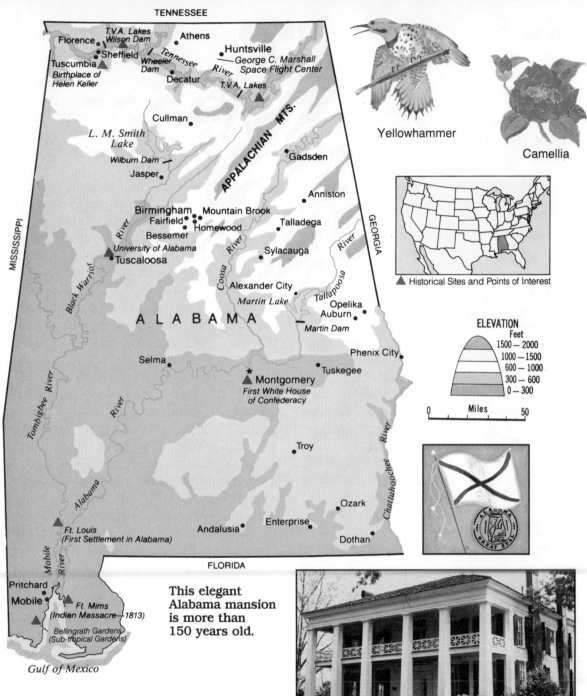

TENNESSEE

Florence
T.V.A. Lakes
Wilson Dam
Sheffield
Tuscumbia
Birthplace of
Helen Keller
Wheeler
Dam
Decatur

Athens

Huntsville
— George C. Marshall
Space Flight Center

Tennessee River

T.V.A. Lakes

Cullman

L. M. Smith Lake

Wilburn Dam

Jasper

APPALACHIAN MTS.

Gadsden

Birmingham
Mountain Brook
Fairfield
Homewood
Bessemer

Anniston

Talladega

University of Alabama
Tuscaloosa

River

Coosa River

Sylacauga

ALABAMA

Alexander City

Martin Lake

Tallapoosa River

Opelika
Auburn

Martin Dam

GEORGIA

MISSISSIPPI

Black Warrior River

Selma

Montgomery
First White House
of Confederacy

Tuskegee

Phenix City

River

Tombigbee River

Alabama River

Troy

Chattahoochee River

Ozark

Andalusia

Enterprise

Dothan

Ft. Louis
(First Settlement in Alabama)

FLORIDA

Pritchard
Mobile

Mobile River

Ft. Mims
(Indian Massacre—1813)

Bellingrath Gardens
(Sub-tropical Gardens)

Gulf of Mexico

Yellowhammer

Camellia

▲ Historical Sites and Points of Interest

ELEVATION
Feet
1500 — 2000
1000 — 1500
600 — 1000
300 — 600
0 — 300

0   Miles   50

This elegant
Alabama mansion
is more than
150 years old.

and marches in the state. His protests helped change the laws in Alabama and helped make life better for black people there. (*See* **King, Martin Luther, Jr.**)

Some remarkable people have lived in Alabama. Helen Keller became both deaf and blind when she was a child. Yet as an adult, she was a famous lecturer and writer.

Booker T. Washington founded Tuskegee Institute. This school for blacks became an important center for finding better ways to grow crops.

George Corley Wallace was Alabama's best-known political figure. He was elected governor four times. W. C. Handy, the "Father of the Blues," was a famous musician. Sports figures born in Alabama include Hank Aaron and Jesse Owens.

Alamo, *see* **Texas**

41

Alaska

Capital: Juneau
Area: 591,004 square miles (1,530,699 square kilometers) (largest state)
Population (1980): 400,481 (1985): about 521,000 (smallest state)
Became a state: January 3, 1959 (49th state)

Alaska is the largest state in the United States, and one of two states that have no borders with any other states. It is a huge region in the northwest corner of North America, bordering Canada and two oceans—the Arctic and the Pacific. It has more land and fewer people than any other state.

The name of the state comes from the Aleut word *alakshak*. The Aleuts are Native Americans who live in Alaska's Aleutian Islands. *Alakshak* means "peninsula" or "great land."

The Land Alaska is indeed a "great land"—so big that the 22 smallest states could fit inside it. Alaska has the 11 highest mountains in the United States. One of them, Mount McKinley, is the highest mountain in all of North America. There are also many glaciers. One, Malaspina, is larger in area than the state of Rhode Island. Alaska is closer to Asia than any other part of the United States. Little Diomede Island, in the Bering Strait, is only 3 miles (5 kilometers) from the Soviet Union.

Alaska has three main parts—a huge heartland and two long arms. The heartland is partly north of the Arctic Circle, and is barren and cold. In the winter, temperatures stay below zero for weeks at a time. The state's longest river, the Yukon, runs through the heartland. The mountains of the Alaskan Range are in the southern part of the region.

Alaska's largest city, Anchorage, is just south of the Alaskan Range. Fairbanks is just north of these mountains. Far to the north, on the shore of the Arctic Ocean, is Barrow, the northernmost settlement in the United States. At Barrow, the sun never rises during midwinter. The coldest temperature ever recorded in the United States was measured near Barrow—80°F (62°C) below zero.

One of Alaska's two arms is a thin strip of land and islands stretching south and east from the heartland, between Canada and the Pacific Ocean. This arm is sometimes called the Panhandle. Weather in the Panhandle is cool and moist. Some parts get 200 inches of rain each year. Juneau, the state capital, is on the Panhandle.

Alaska's second arm stretches away from the heartland to the southwest. It is the long Alaskan Peninsula and the Aleutian Island chain. The peninsula and the islands were formed by volcanoes. Some of them still spout steam and smoke.

History and People Thousands of years ago, Alaska was connected to Asia. People from Asia crossed this "land bridge" looking for food. They were the ancestors of all the Native Americans in North and South America, including Alaska's Aleuts and Eskimo.

The Russians were the first Europeans to see Alaska. Vitus Bering, a Danish explorer who sailed for Russia, sighted Alaska in 1741. Soon after, the Russians built a settlement on Kodiak Island. They ruled Alaska for almost 100 years. They were mostly interested in fur trading.

William Seward, an important person in the U.S. government, wanted the United States to buy Alaska from Russia. Many people laughed at this idea. They called Alaska "Seward's Ice-Box." But Seward got his way. Alaska became a U.S. possession in 1867.

In the late 1890s, thousands of people from the "lower 48" states went to Alaska to look for gold. New towns appeared almost overnight. In 1912, Alaska became a U.S. territory.

During World War II, in the 1940s, thou-

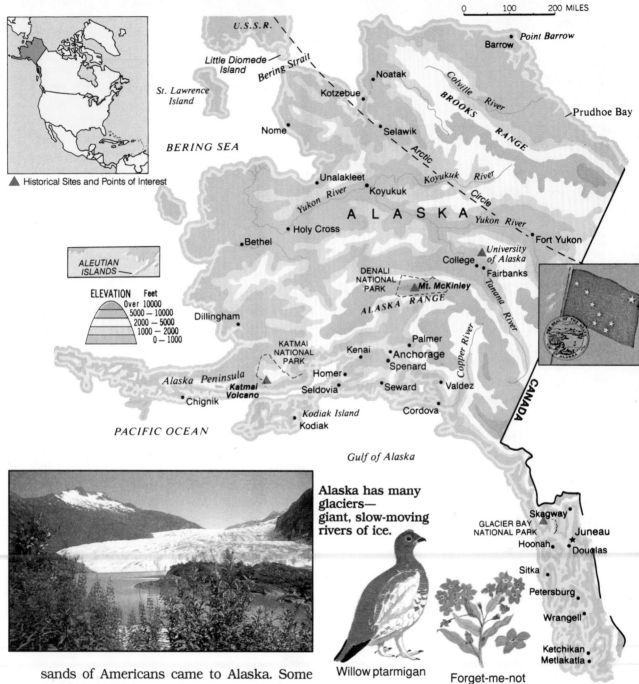

0   100   200 MILES

U.S.S.R.

Point Barrow
Barrow

Little Diomede
Island
Bering Strait

Noatak
Colville River
BROOKS RANGE

St. Lawrence
Island

Kotzebue

Prudhoe Bay

Nome

Selawik

Arctic

Koyukuk River

BERING SEA

Unalakleet
Koyukuk

Circle

Yukon River

A L A S K A

Yukon River

Fort Yukon

▲ Historical Sites and Points of Interest

Holy Cross

Bethel

College
University
of Alaska

DENALI
NATIONAL
PARK
▲ Mt. McKinley
Fairbanks

Tanana River

ALEUTIAN
ISLANDS

ALASKA RANGE

ELEVATION   Feet
Over 10000
5000 – 10000
2000 – 5000
1000 – 2000
0 – 1000

Dillingham

Palmer
Kenai   • Anchorage
Spenard

Copper River

KATMAI
NATIONAL
PARK

Homer

Alaska   Peninsula
Katmai
Volcano ▲

Seldovia
Seward
Valdez

Chignik

Cordova

CANADA

Kodiak Island
Kodiak

PACIFIC OCEAN

Gulf of Alaska

Alaska has many glaciers— giant, slow-moving rivers of ice.

Skagway

GLACIER BAY
NATIONAL PARK ▲

Juneau
Hoonah
Douglas

Sitka

Petersburg

Willow ptarmigan

Forget-me-not

Wrangell

Ketchikan
Metlakatla

sands of Americans came to Alaska. Some decided to stay. Alaska's population grew. In 1959, Alaska became the 49th state.

In the 1960s, oil was discovered in northern Alaska, at Prudhoe Bay. Thousands of workers came to help build a giant oil pipeline from the Arctic Ocean to the Pacific Ocean port of Valdez, near Anchorage. The pipeline began to carry oil across the state in 1977. Lumbering and fishing are also important industries in Alaska.

Alaska has produced important political figures. Ernest Gruening represented the territory of Alaska in Washington, D.C. He urged the U.S. government to make Alaska a state. When statehood came, Gruening was elected to the Senate, where he served until 1969. Walter J. Hickel was governor of Alaska in the 1960s. In 1969, he was appointed secretary of the interior by President Nixon.

Albania, *see* **Europe**

43

Alberta

Capital: Edmonton
Area: 255,285 square miles (661,188 square kilometers) (4th-largest province)
Population (1981): 2,237,724 (1985): about 2,337,500 (4th-largest province)
Became a province: September 1, 1905 (9th province)

Alberta is one of Canada's three Prairie Provinces. It is almost as big as Texas, and most of its land is flat plains and gently rolling prairies. In southwest Alberta, the plains meet the Rocky Mountains, and in the far North are forests and lakes.

The province is named after a princess—Princess Louise Caroline Alberta. Her mother was Queen Victoria of England, and her husband was a governor-general of Canada in the late 1800s.

Land and People Alberta is Canada's fastest-growing province because it has many jobs to offer in two important businesses. Visitors to Alberta soon learn what these businesses are. They often see vast fields of golden wheat dotted with the huge derricks of oil wells. Alberta's major businesses are farming and oil production.

Like the other Prairie Provinces, Alberta produces huge grain crops. In the southern part of the province, fields of wheat, barley, rye, and oats stretch as far as the eye can see. The soil is rich, there is enough rain, and the sun seems to shine almost all the time. In fact, Alberta gets so many hours of sunshine that its nickname is "Sunny Alberta." Farmers in Alberta produce a third of Canada's grain crops and also raise many beef cattle.

Oil has been discovered in many parts of Alberta. In some regions, it is pumped up from underground through wells. In the North, it is taken out of huge deposits of tar sands. Many new oil businesses have been started in Alberta since 1950. Thousands of people have come from other parts of Canada and from other countries to work in these businesses. Nine-tenths of Canada's oil and gas and half of its coal are produced in Alberta.

Edmonton and Calgary are Alberta's two largest cities. More than half of all Albertans live in or near these cities. Edmonton is in central Alberta. It is the capital of the province. The West Edmonton Mall is one of the largest shopping centers in the world.

Calgary is in southwestern Alberta, near the foothills of the Rocky Mountains. In the late 1800s, it was called Fort Calgary and was an outpost of the North-West Mounted Police. It is famous for the Calgary Exhibition and Stampede, a rodeo and fair that goes on for ten days every July.

The rugged Rocky Mountains rise along Alberta's southwestern border with the province of British Columbia. Most of Alberta's mountains are in Banff and Jasper national parks. In Banff, beautiful Lake Louise nestles among majestic, snow-covered peaks. The 1988 Winter Olympic Games were held in the mountains of Alberta.

Far to the north is Wood Buffalo National Park, Canada's largest national park. It extends from Alberta into the neighboring Northwest Territories. The largest herd of buffalo in all of North America roams this park.

Most of northern Alberta is forest and wilderness. Uranium and other minerals are mined there. Many of Alberta's Indians now live in the northern part of the province.

History Indians were the first people to live in what is now Alberta. Blackfoot and other tribes lived on the plains. Cree and others hunted in the forests of the North.

Anthony Henday was probably the first European to reach Alberta. He worked for the Hudson's Bay Company and came in 1754 to trade with the Indians for furs.

In 1870, Canada bought a huge region, in-

A race between chuck wagons is part of the Calgary Stampede, a big celebration held every summer in Alberta's second-largest city.

build forts and to bring law and order to the land. In 1883, the Canadian Pacific Railway reached Calgary. Settlers poured into the region. They set up large ranches and farms.

Alberta was made a province in 1905. About 375,000 people lived there by 1911. Many more new settlers came in the 1950s, after oil and gas were discovered near Edmonton. Today, Alberta has more than 2 million people.

Two Albertans have become prime minister of Canada. Richard B. Bennett was prime minister during the 1930s. Joe Clark was prime minister for nine months in 1979 and 1980. At 39, he was Canada's youngest prime minister. Perhaps the most famous Albertan of all is Wayne Gretzky, who played center for the Edmonton Oilers hockey team and became hockey's greatest scorer.

cluding Alberta, from the Hudson's Bay Company. Alberta was made part of the Northwest Territories. The government sent the North-West Mounted Police to Alberta to

This baby koala is an albino. It has white fur and pink eyes, but its mother's fur is gray.

albino

Albinos are people, animals, or plants that do not have any coloring. True albinos appear white or whitish because their bodies cannot make color pigments. The word *albino* comes from a word that means "white" in Spanish.

Human albinos have no pigment in their skin, hair, or eyes. Their skin is very pale. The blood that flows through the tiny blood vessels in the skin may make it slightly pink. Their hair is snow white. Their eyes are pink, colored only by blood. Without pigment, albinos have no protection against strong light. They quickly sunburn, and their eyes can easily be hurt.

Albinos can be found among many kinds of animals. Some people keep albino rabbits or mice as pets. These animals have white fur and pink eyes.

Albino plants have white leaves. They do not live long because they do not have the green pigment they need to make food. They die when they have used up the food stored in the seeds from which they grew.

Sometimes, only part of a living thing is without pigment. A person may have normal coloring except for one patch of white hair or skin. A bird may have colored feathers except for one white tail feather.

alcohol

Alcohol is the name of a family of chemicals used in medicine, chemistry, and manufacturing. The most familiar is ethyl alcohol, found in alcoholic drinks such as wine, beer, and whiskey. Other alcohols include methyl alcohol and ethylene glycol.

About 3,000 years ago, people learned that grape juice left standing in a warm place for several days becomes bubbly and tastes different. The new liquid has ethyl alcohol in it, and we call it *wine*. People drank it with their meals or during celebrations.

Today, we know how grape juice turns into wine. Tiny, one-celled creatures that can float in the air land in the juice. These creatures, called *yeasts,* eat the sugar in the juice. They turn it into ethyl alcohol and carbon dioxide. Carbon dioxide is a gas and causes the bubbles. Yeasts can also make alcohol from other fruits, from mashed-up grain, and from sugarcane or molasses.

People still drink alcoholic drinks, but we now know that alcohol can be bad for your health. In addition, people who have been drinking alcohol cause many highway accidents. Some people become *alcoholics*—alcohol addicts. (*See* **addiction.**)

Ethyl alcohol has many other uses, however. We use it in medicines, perfumes, cosmetics, and some kinds of paints. It can also be mixed with gasoline to run cars, or used as a fuel by itself.

Another important alcohol is methyl alcohol. Over 200 years ago, people learned to make methyl alcohol from wood. We still often call it *wood alcohol,* even though today it is usually made from crude oil. It is used in plastics and medicines, and in other chemicals. Methyl alcohol is poisonous to drink.

Ethylene glycol is often called *antifreeze* or *coolant.* It is mixed with water and used in car radiators during the winter. People used to put plain water in car radiators. But during winter nights, the water froze and cracked the radiator. Antifreeze protects the car from damage. A mixture of half ethylene

46

glycol and half water does not freeze unless the temperature goes to $-34°F$ ($-37°C$). Ethylene glycol is also poisonous to drink.

In the 1800s, chemists learned that there were many different kinds of alcohol. A molecule of any alcohol is made of carbon atoms, hydrogen atoms, and oxygen atoms. Differences in the number and arrangement of the atoms make one kind of alcohol different from another.

See also **yeast.**

Alcott, Louisa May

Louisa May Alcott is the American author famous for writing *Little Women*. She was born in 1832, over 150 years ago. She spent most of her life in Massachusetts, and died on May 6, 1888.

Her father, Bronson Alcott, was a philosopher, and a friend of many leading writers. The Alcotts were quite poor. Young Louisa decided to help earn money for her family. As a child, she did this by sewing dolls' clothes. When she grew up, she worked as a teacher. She also served as a nurse for the Union Army during the Civil War. Then she became a writer. Her family lived mostly on the money she earned.

Little Women, her most famous book, was published in 1868. It is the story of sisters growing up in New England in the mid-1800s. The parents, Mr. and Mrs. March, have four daughters—Meg, Jo, Beth, and Amy—who plan various ways to make money to support the poor family. The novel tells also of their friends, their loves, and their marriages.

The story was based on Louisa May's own childhood. Jo is like Louisa herself, and Jo's sisters are like Louisa's sisters. The novel was such a success that she wrote other books of the same kind, including *Little Men* and *Jo's Boys.*

See also **children's books.**

Aleutian Islands, *see* Alaska

Louisa May Alcott (bottom) wrote about four sisters (top) in her novel *Little Women.*

Alexander the Great

Alexander the Great was the most powerful military leader and conqueror of ancient times. Before he was 30, he conquered an empire that stretched over 3,000 miles (4,800 kilometers), from Greece to India.

Alexander was born in 356 B.C.—356 years before the birth of Christ—in what is now northern Greece. The region was then called Macedonia. Alexander's father, Philip, was its ruler. Philip hired Aristotle, a famous Greek thinker, to live at his palace and teach Alexander the learning of Greece. For the rest of his life, Alexander admired Greek culture. (*See* **Greece, ancient.**)

When Alexander was 20, his father was killed, and Alexander became king. He then set out to conquer the Persians, who lived in what is now Iran. At this time, the Persians ruled a vast territory. It included not only Persia but also Asia Minor (now Turkey), Syria, Egypt, and lands stretching all the

way to India. The Persian king, Darius, ruled from Persepolis, his capital city.

First, Alexander marched into Asia Minor with about 30,000 troops, most of them Macedonians. In two important battles, he defeated large Persian armies. Then he marched south, taking over the region at the eastern end of the Mediterranean Sea (present-day Syria, Lebanon, and Israel).

Alexander continued into Egypt. The people there were happy to see his invading army, because they hated Persian rule. After Alexander overthrew the Persians in Egypt, he founded a new city, which he named Alexandria. It became a major center of learning and trade. (*See* **Alexandria.**)

In 331 B.C., when he was 25, Alexander began his most famous campaign. He led his forces back from Egypt to Persia, where Darius had again gathered a large army. There was a great battle in which the Persians

Alexander the Great
conquered a huge empire
in ancient times.

EXTENT OF ALEXANDER'S EMPIRE

EUROPE

BLACK SEA

ASIA MINOR

CASPIAN SEA

MEDITERRANEAN SEA

AFRICA

RED SEA

ASIA

0 500 MILES

used their most effective weapons. These were chariots with knives fastened to the wheels, designed to slice into the legs of enemy horses. Alexander won the battle anyway, and the Persians retreated. Soon afterward, Alexander seized Persepolis. When Darius was killed by one of his own generals, Alexander had himself crowned king of Persia.

Alexander then marched hundreds of miles eastward through Persia and into present-day Pakistan. He wanted to go farther, but his men were tired and far from home. They refused to continue. Alexander sailed south along the Indus River to the sea. Then he began the long march home.

Alexander wanted to unify the lands and peoples he had conquered. He wanted to make the many different peoples feel like part of one empire. He introduced the Greek language into many new areas to make communication easier. He made merchants and traders in his empire use Greek money. His army welcomed soldiers of different nationalities. Alexander married a Persian princess and encouraged many other Macedonians to take Persian wives.

Although Alexander was a great conqueror, there was a dark side to his nature. When he defeated a city, he sometimes destroyed every building and sold all the people as slaves. He had a terrible temper, especially when he had been drinking. One night, in a drunken rage, he murdered his closest friend. Alexander admired the Greek idea of rule by the people (democracy), but he was a dictator. He seemed to believe he was a god and wanted everyone to worship him.

When Alexander was only 32, he became ill with malaria. Soon, he realized that he had only a short time to live. He had every Macedonian soldier in his army pass through his tent to say good-bye. Then Alexander died. His baby son was murdered soon afterward. His empire was divided up among his generals, and later it split into many parts. Until modern times, no one was able to conquer such a huge territory again.

Alexandria

Alexandria, a city in Egypt, was founded by the famous conqueror Alexander the Great more than 300 years before the birth of Christ. For many centuries afterward, Alexandria was a major Mediterranean city and the capital of Egypt. Many Greeks lived in the city, and it had a large Jewish community. It was in Alexandria that the Old Testament of the Bible was translated from Hebrew into Greek.

Alexandria was most famous as a center of learning. Its university drew students and scholars from many countries. Its library, the largest in the world at the time, may have had 700,000 volumes.

Alexandria was on the Mediterranean coast. It was an important trading city. In its harbor stood the Pharos, a famous lighthouse. (*See* **Seven Wonders of the World.**)

In the 700s A.D., the Arabs conquered Egypt. They moved the capital from Alexandria to Cairo, and Alexandria became less important. But it is still Egypt's major port and its second-largest city.

See also **Alexander the Great.**

The lighthouse at Alexandria as one artist imagined it.

algae

Algae (AL-jee) are the simplest kinds of plants. An alga (AL-juh) is a single plant or kind of algae. Some algae are large. Others are too small to be seen without a microscope. All algae live in water or damp places and have a very simple body form. Like more complicated plants, algae make their own food from carbon dioxide and water. That process is called *photosynthesis.*

The three major groups of algae are named for their colors—brown, red, and green. Two other groups are sometimes called algae, but they are really not algae at all. They are not even plants. Blue-green "algae" are related to bacteria and are monerans. Golden "algae" are really protists. (*See* **moneran; protist;** and **living things.**)

Brown Algae There are about 1,500 kinds of brown algae. Some grow as long as 50 meters (165 feet). Most brown algae, commonly called *seaweed,* live in the cold parts of oceans. Dead algae often float in to shore and collect along beaches. One common kind of brown algae is kelp. (*See* **kelp.**)

The color of brown algae comes from a brown pigment in their cells. Underneath the brown pigment are green cell parts called *chloroplasts.* These make the algae's food.

Many brown algae are shaped like long, narrow leaves. At one end, a structure that looks like a shallow cup attaches the alga to an underwater rock. That way, the alga cannot float out to sea.

Some brown algae have beadlike parts called *bladders,* which are actually small balloons filled with gases. They help the algae float near the ocean's surface, where they get the most sunlight. Some bladders contain carbon monoxide, a poisonous gas.

Red Algae There are about 4,000 kinds of red algae. Red pigment in their cells hides their green chloroplasts. Most red algae live in the warm parts of oceans. Red algae are generally smaller than brown ones. Like some brown algae, large red algae are some-

times called *seaweed.* Some of them look feathery. Certain red algae can live deeper in the oceans than any other plant—deeper than 120 meters (390 feet).

Green Algae There are about 7,500 kinds of green algae. They are found in both fresh water and salt water. Some green algae are only a single cell. Others are formed of small groups of cells. The cells may line up in chains, or they may form colonies in different shapes.

Some algae have unusual shapes. Large kinds of green algae may be shaped like green fans or leaves. Sea lettuce, one of these species, is found in oceans. Each sea lettuce plant may be as long as 1 meter (3 feet).

Volvox is a green alga that looks like a hollow ball when seen through a microscope. The cells are connected by tiny threads. Each cell also has two threads that help the cell move. The threads of the cells in a *Volvox* colony beat together and make it spin through the water.

Most single-celled green algae can be seen only with a microscope. *Acetabularia* is one kind that you can see without a microscope. It looks a little like a mushroom and can be 2.5 centimeters (1 inch) long.

Uses of Algae Algae provide food and shelter for many living things, in the oceans and in damp soil. In some parts of the ocean, sea algae grow close together and form underwater forests. Like forests on land, they give animals places to live and to have their young. Some fish actually attach their eggs to algae. Other animals feed on it or hide in it to catch other animals.

Humans, too, use algae in a number of ways. Some red and brown algae are used in Japanese and Chinese cooking. Other kinds are used as a topping for vegetables or as a wrapping for rice or raw fish. Some kinds are even eaten like candy.

Some chemicals made from algae are used in foods, such as ice cream, cheese, chocolate milk, and jellies. We use other chemicals from algae in paint, printer's ink, soap, toothpaste, and buttons. Some brown algae

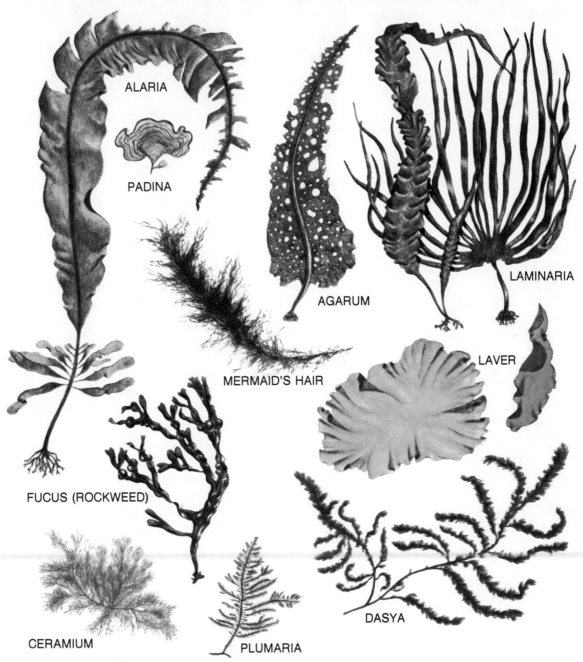

ALARIA

PADINA

AGARUM

LAMINARIA

MERMAID'S HAIR

LAVER

FUCUS (ROCKWEED)

DASYA

CERAMIUM

PLUMARIA

Algae come in many shapes, colors, and sizes. Some kinds provide important food for sea creatures.

are chopped up and used to enrich soil for crops. Red algae is a source of a jellylike substance called *agar*. Scientists grow microscopic living things in agar.

Special ships harvest some kinds of algae. As the ships move through seaweed beds, workers chop off the tops of the plants. The plants grow from the bottom and quickly replace the parts that have been cut off. In one day, some seaweeds can grow one-third to two-thirds of a meter (1 to 2 feet).

Research in outer space presents a new use for algae. Spacecraft are rather small, and a full-size plant can take up a lot of room. However, thousands of one-celled algae can be brought along in a small jar. Many plant experiments have been done in space using one-celled green algae, especially an alga named *Chlorella.*

See also **photosynthesis.**

algebra

Algebra is the part of mathematics that deals with unknown numbers. It uses special ways to find unknown numbers.

Algebra uses letters or pictures called *symbols* to take the place of unknown numbers. For example, suppose your friend has some cookies but won't tell you how many. You can use the letter *C* in place of the number. You can say your friend has *C* cookies. When you finally find out how many cookies your friend has, you will know what number *C* equals.

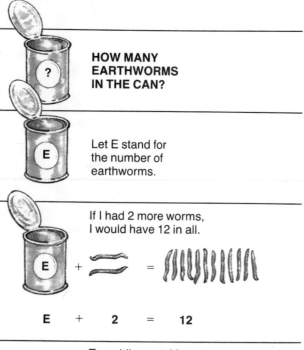

HOW MANY EARTHWORMS IN THE CAN?

Let E stand for the number of earthworms.

If I had 2 more worms, I would have 12 in all.

E + 2 = 12

Try adding or taking away the same number from both sides of the equal sign. Take away 2 from each side.

E + 2 − 2 = 12 − 2
E = 10

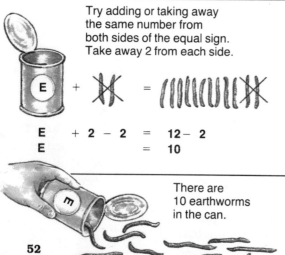

There are 10 earthworms in the can.

Imagine that you know that if you find two more earthworms, you will have 12 of them—but you cannot remember how many earthworms you have now. Algebra will help you find out.

Let *E* stand for the number of earthworms you have. Then *E* plus 2 must be 12. In algebra, you write $E + 2 = 12$. This is called an *equation*—an algebra statement that says two things are equal, or the same. The equation shows the information you know and uses symbols to stand for numbers you do not yet know.

How do you find out what number *E* stands for? This is called *solving* the equation, which is like balancing a seesaw. When you add or subtract something on one side, you must do exactly the same on the other side or the sides will not be equal.

To solve $E + 2 = 12$, try adding or subtracting something on both sides—something that will leave *E* all alone on one side. In this case, for example, try subtracting 2 from both sides. (The seesaw will still balance, because you've done the same thing to each side.) Now you have $E = 10$. That's it! You're finished. $E = 10$ is called the *solution* of the equation. It tells you that you have 10 earthworms.

Here's the way the equation and its solution are written in algebra:

$$E + 2 \qquad = 12$$
$$E + 2 - 2 = 12 - 2$$
$$E \qquad\quad = 10$$

Algebra is an important part of mathematics. You can use equations to make statements about all numbers as well as to solve problems. For example, here are some equations that work for all numbers:

$$X + 0 = X$$
$$X \times 1 = X$$

The first equation shows that adding 0 to a number will not change the number. For example, $5 + 0$ still equals 5. The second shows that multiplying a number by 1 does not change the number. For example, 7×1 still equals 7.

See also **mathematics.**

People gather at a marketplace in Algeria.

Algeria

Capital: Algiers
Area: 919,591 square miles (2,381,592 square kilometers)
Population (1985): about 22,107,000
Official language: Arabic

Algeria is a country in North Africa. It faces the Mediterranean Sea. Algeria is a big country, about one-quarter the size of the United States.

The Sahara covers the southern nine-tenths of the country. Very little rain falls in the Sahara. A few people live there in *oases* —places where water from springs or wells makes the land fertile. A few others work in desert oil fields. But the two largest cities, Algiers and Oran, are both ports on the Mediterranean Sea. Most Algerians live near the Mediterranean shore.

Most Algerians are Arabs or Berbers. Like most of the people of North Africa and the Middle East, they are Muslims—people who follow the Islamic religion.

Almost a third of Algeria's people are farmers. Most of the farms are within 100 miles (160 kilometers) of the coast. Grain, grapes, tobacco, citrus fruits, olives, and figs are important crops. But a large percent of the country's money comes from producing oil and natural gas, most of which is sold to other countries.

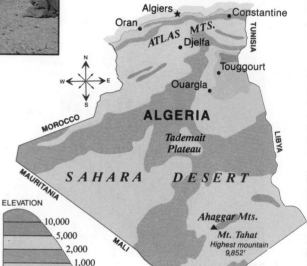

Berbers are the first people known to have lived in Algeria. They were nomads who roamed the deserts of North Africa nearly 4,000 years ago. The Berbers were conquered and ruled by the Phoenicians and later by the Romans. In the 500s A.D., the Arabs conquered the region. They ruled for 900 years. Then the Turks ruled for another 300 years.

In the mid-1800s, the French took control of Algeria and made it a colony. During that time, many French people lived in Algeria. But in the 1950s, the Algerians demanded their independence. They fought a bitter war against the French. Finally, in 1962, Algeria became an independent country.

Many Algerians are poor. Today, the government is using money from the sale of Algeria's oil to build schools and factories to give poor Algerians better education and better jobs.

See also **Islam** and **Sahara**.

Muhammad Ali (left) fights Joe Frazier for the heavyweight championship of the world.

Ali, Muhammad

Muhammad Ali was a great American boxer of the 1960s and 1970s. He was the first boxer to win the world heavyweight championship three different times. Yet boxing was just one reason Ali became one of the most recognized people in the world.

Ali was born in 1942, in Louisville, Kentucky. His parents gave him the name Cassius Clay, Jr. At age 18, he won an Olympic gold medal in boxing. Four years later, in 1964, he won the world heavyweight championship by defeating Sonny Liston.

Unlike many heavyweight boxers, young Ali was light on his feet and quick with his hands. He said that he could "float like a butterfly, sting like a bee." Ali made up poems about his fights and bragged about how he would beat his opponents. Sometimes, before a fight, he told everyone what round he would knock out the other boxer. He called himself "The Greatest."

After becoming the champion, he joined the Black Muslims, a group that believes in the Islamic religion. He took Muhammad Ali as his Muslim name.

In 1967, Ali refused to go into the United States Army when he was drafted. He said war was against his religious beliefs. This angered many people. Officials took away his championship and would not let him box. A court in Texas tried to send him to jail for refusing to be drafted.

In 1971, the U.S. Supreme Court ruled that Ali had broken no law. He was allowed to box again, and three years later he won the championship back. He fought in Africa and Asia as well as America and became a hero to millions around the world.

After Ali retired in 1979, there were other heavyweight champions. But none of them became as popular as Ali. For many people, he was still "The Greatest."

See also boxing.

Alice in Wonderland

More than 100 years ago, Lewis Carroll made up an amazing story to entertain some children on a picnic. He told them about a young girl who followed a rabbit down a hole in the ground and found herself in Wonderland. He named the girl Alice, after Alice Liddell, one of his young listeners. He called the story *Alice in Wonderland*.

One of Alice's adventures takes place at a tea party. First, Alice meets the Mad Hatter. He asks riddles that have no answers. The March Hare offers her wine, but doesn't have any to give her. The Dormouse falls asleep in the middle of speaking. The Cheshire Cat is another strange Wonderland character. He can make himself vanish in bits and pieces, leaving behind only his eerie smile floating in the air.

The Queen of Hearts is cruel but funny. She makes everyone play croquet using flamingos for mallets and hedgehogs for balls. When anyone displeases the Queen, she shouts, "Off with her head!"

Alice hears the Queen of Hearts shout "Off with her head!"

Alice's adventures end when she realizes that the annoying characters are "nothing but a pack of cards."

Children liked Lewis Carroll's story, so he published it as a book. Seven years later, he published another story about Alice called *Through the Looking-Glass.*

See also **Carroll, Lewis.**

allergy

When some people breathe in ragweed pollen, their eyes begin to itch, their noses run, and they begin to sneeze. These people have an allergy to ragweed pollen. Other kinds of allergies can cause a person to break out in a rash or even to have trouble breathing.

An allergy is an abnormal reaction to some particular substance. The substance that causes the reaction is called an *allergen.* There are four major ways allergens can enter our systems: through the air we breathe, through what we eat, through injections into our bodies (such as insect bites or drug injections), and through contact with our skin.

Some allergens float in the air. Many people are allergic to *pollen grains*—tiny particles released by flowering plants. Most pollen grains are too small to see. When a plant releases them, they float through the air. We all breathe in pollen, but most people never notice that the pollen is there. Only people who are allergic to a certain pollen get itchy eyes or runny noses. Pollen allergies are sometimes called *hay fever.*

Foods sometimes cause allergies. If you are allergic to a food, it may upset your stomach and make your skin break out in red bumps called *hives.* Chocolate, nuts, and eggs are foods that some people are allergic to.

A small number of people are allergic to bee stings or to injections of a particular drug, such as penicillin. Since the allergen goes straight into the bloodstream, these allergies can cause strong symptoms such as difficulty in breathing. People who have such allergies must be especially careful to avoid the substance they are allergic to.

Things we touch may cause allergic reactions. A person who is allergic to dogs or cats may get hives or watery eyes or begin sneezing if he or she pets a dog or cat. Poison oak and poison ivy often act as allergens.

Most allergies are annoying but not serious. Yet a severe allergic reaction can be dangerous. If a person has a severe allergic reaction, he or she should get medical care as soon as possible. Mild allergies can be controlled most easily by staying away from the allergen that causes the reaction.

Scientists are not sure why some people are allergic to things that are harmless to the rest of us. Part of the answer may be that we can inherit an allergy from our parents. People in the same family often have allergies to the same things.

About one person in nine has an allergy of some kind.

poison ivy

ragweed

strawberry

feather

cat

Many alligators live in the Everglades in southern Florida.

alligators and crocodiles

Alligators and crocodiles are large reptiles with strong jaws. They live in warm water and swim very well. Both animals have long bodies and four short legs. Some crocodiles are more than 7 meters (23 feet) long! Their flat tails make up more than half their length. Some alligators can grow as long as 6 meters (20 feet), but most full-grown ones are usually about 3 meters (10 feet) long.

Like all reptiles, alligators and crocodiles breathe air and have a backbone and dry, scaly skin. They are related to each other and are distant relatives of snakes, lizards, and turtles.

Alligators and crocodiles look very much alike. In general, alligators have shorter snouts than crocodiles. An alligator's row of lower teeth fits behind its row of upper teeth. When the alligator's jaws are closed, only the upper teeth can be seen. A crocodile's teeth meet. You can see a large bottom tooth on each side when the jaws are closed.

Scientists believe that crocodiles and alligators were among the earliest reptiles. Fossils of some crocodiles have been found that may be 235 million years old. Those ancient crocodiles were much like crocodiles today.

Where They Live Alligators and crocodiles are found only in warm areas, since they cannot live in cold waters. When water temperatures fall below 65° F (18° C), a crocodile will sink and drown.

Alligators live in only two places, the Yangtze River valley in China and the southeastern United States. Crocodiles are found in many warm regions. A few live in southern Florida (where alligators also live). Others are found in South and Central America, Africa, Asia, and Australia.

Alligators live only in fresh water—rivers, lakes, and swamps. Most crocodiles live in fresh water, but they may swim out to sea for short periods of time. Only one kind of crocodile, which lives in the Indian Ocean, stays in salt water for long periods of time.

Finding and Eating Food The dark, dull greenish brown color of alligators and crocodiles blends with the muddy background of a slow-moving river. They swim with most of their bodies underwater. Only their eyes, ears, and nostrils are above the surface. The animals they are stalking often do not notice them until it is too late.

Alligators and crocodiles are carnivores—meat-eaters. The young eat mostly insects, crabs, and tiny fish. As they grow, they eat fewer insects and more fish. Full-grown alligators and crocodiles also eat rats, birds, and larger animals. They lie in wait near places where deer, wild pigs, and other large animals like to drink. When a careless animal stands too close to the water's edge and bends to drink, the alligator or crocodile catches the animal in its jaws and drags it into the water. It holds the animal under the water until it drowns.

Alligators and crocodiles have stones and pebbles in their stomachs. Scientists think the stones help the animals grind up food so that it can be digested. The animals may swallow other objects if they cannot find stones. Some have swallowed glass bottles and parts of guns.

Nests and Young When female alligators or crocodiles are ready to lay eggs, they find shady spots on land near the water. Some dig a hole in the sand, lay the eggs, and cover them. Others build a large mound from mud and leaves. They lay the eggs in a shallow hole in the mound, then put more leaves over the eggs. The female stays near the nest, guarding it against enemies.

After several months, the young are ready to hatch. They begin to peep loudly. Their mother hears them and uncovers the eggs so that the young can get out of the nest.

For a while, young alligators and crocodiles stay near their mothers. Then they go off on their own. Many are eaten by fish, birds, or mammals. Few survive to become full-grown adults.

Contact with Humans Alligators and crocodiles usually move slowly, but they can move very quickly in times of danger. Most of the time, they run away from people. But if they are cornered or if they are guarding their young, they may attack. The muscles alligators and crocodiles use to shut their jaws are very powerful. But the muscles they use to open their jaws are rather weak. Once

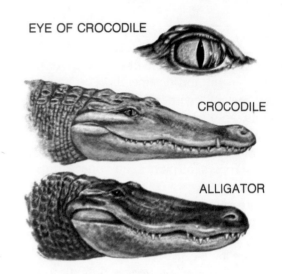

EYE OF CROCODILE

CROCODILE

ALLIGATOR

Alligators and crocodiles have different snouts. You can tell the crocodile by the large bottom tooth.

the jaws are closed, an adult human can usually hold them shut.

Humans kill many alligators and crocodiles. We use their skin to make handbags, shoes, and other goods. Humans have also taken away the animals' homes by draining swamps. Alligators and crocodiles are now protected by law in many places.

Caimans and Gavials Caimans and gavials are related to crocodiles and alligators. Caimans closely resemble alligators. They live in northern South America. Gavials live in rivers in India. They have long, thin snouts and more than 100 teeth. They spend almost all their time in water.

See also **reptile.**

Crocodiles move slowly on land, but are powerful swimmers.

alloy

An alloy is a mixture of two or more metals or of metal and nonmetals. The ingredients are melted together. When the mixture hardens, an alloy is formed. It is different from any of the materials that were used to make it. Modern alloys are important in building skyscrapers, airplanes, and spaceships.

Early Alloys People discovered how to make alloys long ago, before the beginning of recorded time. Bronze, the first important alloy made by man, changed human history. Before its use, people made tools from stones or from copper. Stone was difficult to shape. Copper was easy to shape, but it was also easy to dent. About 5,500 years ago, in the Middle East, metalworkers learned to melt copper and add a small amount of tin. The new alloy, bronze, was stronger than either copper or tin. People used bronze to make long-lasting cups, cooking pots, hammers, swords, armor, shields, chariots, large doors, hoes, wheels, and statues.

About 3,000 years later, the Romans discovered another important alloy, brass. This mixture of copper and zinc is shinier and softer than bronze. Decorative pots, plates, picture frames, locks, keys, and door knockers are still made from brass.

Amalgam is a third ancient alloy. Many people carry amalgam with them all the time—in the fillings of their teeth. Amalgam contains mercury and other metals. The Romans and Greeks discovered mercury—the only metal that is liquid at room temperature—and found that they could easily dissolve small amounts of silver, gold, and tin in it, forming the alloy. When amalgam is warm, it is soft and easy to shape. Dentists can press it firmly into a cavity. When it cools, it hardens and makes the tooth almost as good as new.

CAUTION: Amalgams are not dangerous, but liquid mercury is very poisonous. Do not try to make an amalgam yourself.

Modern Alloys These early discoveries have helped scientists create thousands of new alloys. We see or use some every day.

Today, steel is probably the most useful alloy. Metalworkers make it by adding a small amount of carbon to melted iron. Steel is stronger and more flexible than iron. When small amounts of nickel and chromium are added to steel, they produce stainless steel. This alloy resists rusting, is extremely

An ancient brass coin and a modern jet engine are both made of alloys.

strong, and is used to build skyscrapers, ships, factories, railroad cars, and bridges. Stainless steel is also used to make spoons, forks, knives, and other kitchen utensils.

Alloys of aluminum have helped build sturdy, lightweight jet planes and space stations. Aluminum alloys often include small amounts of magnesium, which makes them as strong as steel. Yet these alloys weigh only a third as much as the same volume of steel.

There are many alloys of silver and gold. Sterling silver is a mixture of silver and copper. Shiny sterling silver candlesticks, trays, and jewelry are much stronger than those made from silver alone. Gold jewelry is usually made of a gold alloy, because pure gold is soft and would bend or scratch too easily.

Alloys have been important to people from prehistoric times into the space age. When you see a gold ring, an airplane, a skyscraper, or even a penny, remember that alloys help make them possible.

See also **bronze** and **metal**.

almanac

An almanac is a book filled with information on all kinds of subjects, from movies to postage to weather. Most almanacs are published once a year, with new information added.

You can use an almanac to find out which teams have won a World Series, the population of any state or country, the birthdays of famous people, and many other things.

The first almanacs were made thousands of years ago and were like calendars. They had information about the seasons and important holidays, and about the moon and stars. The oldest almanac that still exists was written in the 1200s.

One of the first books printed in America was an almanac for the year 1639. The most famous American almanac was *Poor Richard's Almanack*, which Benjamin Franklin first printed in 1732. It included wise sayings that Franklin had heard or made up.

The Old Farmer's Almanack is an almanac that predicts what the weather will be

WORLD FLAGS and

AFGHANISTAN
ALBANIA
ALGERIA
ANGOLA
ANTIGUA & BARBUDA
ARGENTINA
AUSTRALIA
AUSTRIA

352   Awards — Nobel, Pulitzer Prizes

Peace

1985 Intl. Physicians for the Prevention of Nuclear War, U.S.
1984 Bishop Desmond Tutu, So. African
1983 Lech Walesa, Polish
1982 Alva Myrdal, Swedish; Alfonso Garcia Robles, Mexican
1981 Office of U.N. High Commissioner for Refugees
1980 Adolfo Perez Esquivel, Argentine
1979 Mother Teresa of Calcutta, Albanian-Indian
1978 Anwar Sadat, Egyptian Menachem Begin, Israeli
1977 Amnesty International
1976 Mairead Corrigan, Betty Williams, N. Irish
1975 Andrei Sakharov, USSR
1974 Eisaku Sato, Japanese, Sean MacBride, Irish
1973 Henry Kissinger, U.S. Le Duc Tho, N. Vietnamese (Tho declined)
1971 Willy Brandt, W. German

1960 Albert J. Luthuli, South African
1959 Philip J. Noel-Baker, British
1958 Georges Pire, Belgian
1957 Lester B. Pearson, Canadian
1954 Office of the UN High Commissioner for Refugees
1953 George C. Marshall, U.S.
1952 Albert Schweitzer, French
1951 Leon Jouhaux, French
1950 Ralph J. Bunche, U.S.
1949 Lord John Boyd Orr of Brechin Mearns, British
1947 Friends Service Council, Brit. Amer. Friends Service Com.
1946 Emily G. Balch, John R. Mott, both U.S.
1945 Cordell Hull, U.S.
1944 International Red Cross
1938 Nansen International Office for Refugees
1937 Viscount Cecil of Chelwood, Brit.
1936 Carlos

An almanac is published every year, so the information is up-to-date.

for each day in the coming year. It also tells farmers and gardeners the best times to plant their crops.

alphabet

An alphabet is a set of symbols called *letters*. A letter stands for a particular sound. When several letters are put together, they make up a word. For example, the word *bit* uses three symbols, *b*, *i*, and *t*, to show the three sounds in the word.

The English alphabet has 26 letters, some of them standing for more than one sound. For example, the letter *k* always stands for the same sound, but the letter *c* stands for different sounds. It has two different sounds

59

in the word *circle*. We also show some sounds by combinations of letters. For example, the *ch* in *children* stands for a special sound for which there is no separate letter.

How Alphabets Developed The first systems of writing were not alphabets. They used simple pictures to stand for things. For example, one picture might stand for "ox," another for "man," and another for "house." Later, pictures were added that stood for ideas. People do something like this now when they use a drawing of a red heart to mean "love."

Drawing a picture for each word was very slow, so writers began to make simpler drawings, called *symbols*. After many centuries, there was a symbol for each word. In order to read or write this kind of picture writing, people must learn the symbols for all the words in their language. This can take years.

The Chinese still use a system of picture writing. There are many different spoken languages in China, but there is only one written language. Chinese people may have

In Egyptian writing, one symbol stands for a word, a syllable, or a sound.

different words for "horse," but they all recognize the written symbol for "horse."

The ancient Egyptians also used picture writing. When a word had two syllables, they sometimes drew two symbols, one for each syllable. We would be doing something like this if we wrote the word *season* by drawing a symbol for "sea" and a symbol for "sun."

Soon, there were other languages that used symbols for each syllable of a word. The ancient Semites, who lived in the Middle East, developed a kind of syllable writing. Hebrew, one of the languages of the Bible, was written in this way. In Japan today, there are two systems of writing. One is a kind of picture writing like that of China. The other is a system of syllable writing, which is easier to learn.

The Phoenicians, who came from the eastern shore of the Mediterranean Sea, developed the first real alphabet. They used picture writing and syllable writing, but they used only 22 symbols for all the sounds. Many of their symbols are like the letters we use in English today.

The ancient Greeks changed the 22 Phoenician symbols into the Greek alphabet. Our English word *alphabet* comes from the first two letters of the Greek alphabet, *alpha* (*A*) and *beta* (*B*). The ancient Romans took the Greek alphabet and turned it into one that fit their own language, using 23 letters instead of 22.

The English Alphabet The early English took their alphabet from the Romans, but added three letters, for a total of 26. The Roman letter *I* could be either a vowel or a consonant. In the English alphabet, *I* is used for vowel sounds, and *J* is used for consonant sounds. The Roman letter *V* could also be a vowel or a consonant. In the English alphabet, *V* is for a consonant sound and *U* is for vowel sounds. A sound that the Romans showed by writing *VV* became the new English letter *W*.

Many letters in our alphabet can be traced all the way back to symbols used in picture writing. For example, the letter *A* can be

Arabic
Hebrew →
ΚΑΛΩΣ ΩΡΙΣΑΤΕ
Modern Greek →
Bengali →
WELCOME
English →
Chinese ↓

People use many writing systems. These signs all say the same thing. Arrows show which way they read.

traced to a Phoenician symbol for "ox."

The letters of the alphabet are arranged in a particular order. This is called *alphabetical order.* Encyclopedias, dictionaries, and phone books are all arranged in this order. If you know alphabetical order, you can look up any word or name you want to learn about.

Other Alphabets Many languages—including Spanish, French, Italian, and German—use most of the same Roman letters we use in English. The letters do not always stand for the same sounds, however. Certain letters may have accents or other special marks over their tops.

The Greek alphabet has some of the letters we know in English and some unfamiliar letters. The Russian alphabet is based on the Greek alphabet and also has several unfamiliar letters.

Arabic and Hebrew use different symbols for the letters in their alphabets, and write them from right to left. Some countries in Africa and Asia have changed the Roman alphabet to fit their own languages.

Alps

The Alps, the largest chain of mountains on the continent of Europe, cover parts of France, Italy, Switzerland, West Germany, Austria, Yugoslavia, and Albania. The Alps chain is shaped like a half-circle and is about 750 miles (1,200 kilometers) long.

Hundreds of peaks in the Alps are more than 10,000 feet (3,000 meters) above sea level. Mont Blanc, on the border between Italy and France, is the highest peak. It towers 15,771 feet (4,807 meters) high. The Matterhorn and the Jungfrau are other famous peaks. Several rivers begin high in the Alps, including the Rhine and the Danube.

Ice and snow cover the tops of the Alps all year. There are more than a thousand *glaciers*—flowing rivers of ice. Sometimes, there are avalanches, in which huge masses of snow fall and slide down the steep mountain slopes. (*See* **avalanche.**)

People from around the world come to see the mountains and beautiful green valleys. They also come to ski or to go mountain climbing. The Winter Olympic Games have been held in the Alps a number of times.

For centuries, travelers have followed natural passes through the mountains. One famous pass is the Great St. Bernard Pass between Switzerland and Italy. For more than 1,000 years, monks have bred and trained large St. Bernard dogs to rescue people who get stranded or lost.

The railroads and highways through the Alps also follow the passes. Tunnels through

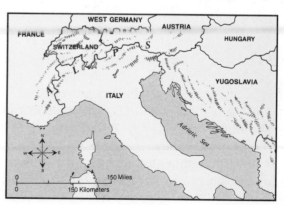

A green valley in the middle
of the Swiss Alps.

the mountains make travel easier and faster. The Simplon railroad tunnel between Italy and Switzerland is more than 12 miles (19 kilometers) long. The longest highway tunnel in the world is the Mont Blanc tunnel between Italy and France. It is more than 7 miles (11 kilometers) long.

aluminum

Aluminum is a shiny metal that is used to make hundreds of everyday items. Aluminum foil, aluminum pots and pans, and soft-drink cans are found in almost every home. Aluminum is also the most important metal used to build airplanes, spaceships, and satellites.

Pure aluminum is soft, but it can be made as strong as steel by mixing it with other metals. Aluminum is much lighter than steel. A cubic foot of steel weighs about 227 kilograms (500 pounds), but a cubic foot of aluminum weighs only 77 kilograms (170 pounds). (*See* **alloy.**)

Minerals containing aluminum are found in dirt, stone, and clay all over the world. But it is difficult to separate the aluminum from the minerals. Scientists first produced pure aluminum in 1825. In 1855, it was still so rare that a piece of aluminum was displayed in a case at the world's fair in Paris.

In 1886, scientists found an efficient way to produce pure aluminum from an ore called *bauxite.* The largest bauxite mines are in the countries of Jamaica and Indonesia. Much of the bauxite is shipped to the United States to be made into aluminum. Making aluminum takes huge amounts of electricity. Aluminum companies save energy and raw materials by recycling scrap aluminum, including aluminum cans.

See also **metal.**

Amazon River

The Amazon, in South America, is the second-longest river in the world. It is about 4,000 miles (6,400 kilometers) long. Only the Nile River in Africa is longer.

The Amazon begins as a small stream high in the Andes Mountains in Peru. As it

flows eastward across Brazil, hundreds of other rivers and streams flow into it. The river becomes wide and deep. By the time the Amazon empties into the Atlantic Ocean, it is carrying more water than any other river in the world. In fact, the Amazon carries more than one-tenth of all the world's flow of water into the sea. The force of the flow is so great that the river's muddy waters can be seen in the Atlantic 200 miles (320 kilometers) from shore.

At some points, the Amazon is 6 miles (10 kilometers) wide. Oceangoing ships can travel all the way upriver to Iquitos, Peru. Iquitos is 2,300 miles (3,700 kilometers) from the Atlantic.

The Amazon and the rivers that flow into it drain more than one-third of South America. Most of this area, called the Amazon basin, is part of the world's largest tropical rain forest. More than 40,000 kinds of plants and trees grow in the forest. Monkeys, anteaters, crocodiles, anacondas, and many other kinds of animals live there. The river itself is home to the piranha, a fierce flesh-eating fish. (*See* **rain forest**.)

Indians live in the rain forest and along the river. When Spanish explorers discovered the river in the 1500s, they were attacked by women warriors from an Indian village. The explorers remembered a Greek legend about women warriors called Amazons, and so they named the river the Amazon.

ameba

An ameba (*a-MEE-ba*) is a one-celled living thing. It has no one lasting shape because its jellylike form changes as it moves. Most amebas can be seen only through a microscope, though one very large kind of ameba can be seen with the naked eye.

Amebas move in an unusual way. Part of the ameba flows forward, forming what is called a *false foot*. The rest of the ameba follows. More false feet form, and the ameba moves some more. This motion makes the ameba look like it is gliding along a surface. False feet also help amebas gather food. Amebas eat other one-celled living things, such as bacteria and algae. A false foot flows around the food and traps it inside the

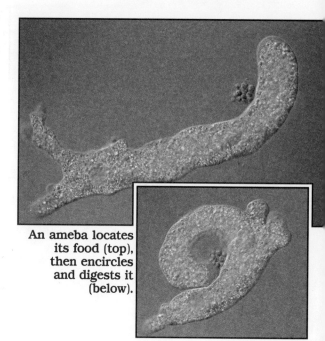

An ameba locates its food (top), then encircles and digests it (below).

ameba. Then the ameba digests the food and uses it for energy.

Amebas reproduce by splitting into two new cells in a process called *binary fission.* The new cells are only half the size of the parent cell that divided. These new amebas grow until they are full-size. Then they, too, divide to form more amebas.

There are many kinds of amebas. They live in fresh water, in salt water, in the soil, and even inside humans and other animals. Most amebas are harmless, but a few can cause serious diseases.

See also **moneran.**

America, *see* United States; North America; South America; Central America

American history, *see* United States history

American Revolution, *see* Revolutionary War

Some great American storytellers: Mark Twain, Jack London, Ernest Hemingway . . .

American writers

Some people write things to be printed and sold in books or magazines. Of these, a few become famous for their writings. Many Americans became famous writers. People all around the world read their books, stories, and poems.

There are many different kinds of writing. Some writers write stories to entertain their readers. Others write poetry. Still others write speeches and essays about important subjects.

Stories When we think of famous writers, we think first of storytellers—writers of stories and novels. A novel is a long story. It may be 100 or even 1,000 pages long. A writer of novels is called a *novelist.*

Some of America's great novelists told new kinds of stories. Some wrote about the wilderness and about American Indians. In

the early 1800s, James Fenimore Cooper wrote about a woodsman named Natty Bumppo. Natty lived on the edge of the wilderness in New York State. He knew the Indians, and he helped new settlers. The most famous book about Natty Bumppo is called *The Deerslayer.*

Later, other writers told stories about pioneers who were settling in the wilderness. One of the greatest of these writers was Mark Twain. He traveled in California and Nevada in the late 1800s and wrote stories about miners who were digging for gold and silver.

Mark Twain also wrote about growing up in a small town on the Mississippi River. He grew up in such a town himself, and he remembered what it was like. In *Tom Sawyer,* he wrote about a mischievous boy and his friends who have exciting adventures. Later, he wrote *The Adventures of Huckleberry*

. . . and Edgar Allan Poe.

Finn, about another boy in the same town who ran away by floating down the Mississippi on a raft. (*See* **Twain, Mark.**)

Later, a writer named Jack London went to northern Canada, where miners were digging for gold. He wrote stories about their adventures. His most famous story, *Call of the Wild,* is about a dog in the Far North who is forced to become wild and live with wolves. (*See* **London, Jack.**)

Herman Melville was another writer who told stories of adventure. Many of his stories were about the sea, and about seamen who traveled to distant parts of the world. His great novel *Moby Dick* is named for a huge white whale. Ahab, the captain of a whaling ship, wants to kill Moby Dick. Ahab wants to catch the whale so badly that he finally destroys himself and his ship.

In the 1900s, Ernest Hemingway wrote great adventure stories. He fought in a war in Spain, went hunting for big game in Africa, and lived in many parts of the world. One of his novels, *The Old Man and the Sea,* is about a brave Cuban fisherman.

Not all storytellers wrote adventure stories. Others described how people learn about good and evil. Nathaniel Hawthorne was a great novelist in the 1800s. Many of the characters in his books have done something wrong and are looking for forgiveness.

Edgar Allan Poe was another writer whose work is about good and evil. He was one of the first writers of horror stories. In one, "The Tell-Tale Heart," a murderer thinks he can hear the dead man's heart beating. He is so frightened that he confesses to the murder. Then he discovers that the "heartbeat" is really only the ticking of his watch. Poe also wrote one of the first detective stories, "The Murders in the Rue Morgue," in which an investigator solves a crime.

Poets People sometimes love to read poetry or to hear it read aloud. There have been many famous American poets. One of the first was Anne Bradstreet, who lived from 1612 to 1672. She came to New England with the early settlers from England. She wrote poems about God, about her family, and about day-to-day life.

Henry Wadsworth Longfellow was a popular poet who wrote long poems about events in American history. *The Song of Hiawatha,* about an Indian ruler, makes use of American Indian tales. *The Courtship of Miles Standish* tells a love story from colonial times.

Longfellow's most famous short poem is "Paul Revere's Ride." It tells how Paul Revere galloped from Boston to warn people in the countryside that the British army was coming. The people got ready, and the next day, they fought the first battle of the Revolutionary War.

Walt Whitman was one of America's greatest poets. He wrote a new kind of poetry,

Three American poets: Robert Frost, Emily Dickinson, and Walt Whitman.

which did not rhyme and had no regular rhythm. Whitman grew up in Brooklyn, New York. During the Civil War, he worked as a nurse, helping wounded soldiers from both sides. For most of his life, he worked on one book of poems, called *Leaves of Grass.* He first published it in 1855. Every few years, he added more poems and published *Leaves of Grass* again. At first, many people did not like Whitman's poetry. In time, people came to see that he was a great poet.

Another poet was writing at about the same time as Whitman. No one knew about her poems, however, because she kept the poems hidden away. Emily Dickinson was very shy. For most of her life, she hardly ever left her house. There she wrote wonderful short poems about love, life, and death. After she died, her poetry was published. People were surprised to find that this shy woman was a very fine poet.

In the 1900s, Robert Frost was one of America's most famous poets. Many of his poems were about country life. Frost grew up in New England and lived on farms there for many years. Two of his famous poems are "Birches" and "The Road Not Taken."

Speeches and Essays In the 1600s and 1700s, many American books were about religion. Most of the writers were ministers. Others wrote histories of their colonies.

In the late 1700s, many writings were about government. The people in America were unhappy being ruled by the government of Britain. Some of them wanted America to have a government of its own.

Patrick Henry, a Virginian, became famous for a speech against the British government. It ended, "Give me liberty or give me death!" (*See* **Henry, Patrick.**)

In 1776, Thomas Jefferson wrote the Declaration of Independence. It told the world that the colonies in America were becoming a new, independent country. Jefferson later became the third president of the new United States. (*See* **Jefferson, Thomas.**)

Another famous writer of that time was Benjamin Franklin. Later, he became a scientist, inventor, and government leader. But he started out as a writer and printer. One book that he published each year was *Poor Richard's Almanack.* Franklin wrote many things in the almanacs. He collected or made up short sayings for them. Franklin also wrote his *Autobiography,* the story of his own life. (*See* **Franklin, Benjamin.**)

Henry David Thoreau was a writer who loved the outdoors. For two years, two months, and two days he lived alone in a small cabin by a pond in Massachusetts. Later, he wrote about his life by the pond in a book called *Walden.* He told what he had learned about the outdoors and about himself.

Abraham Lincoln was president of the United States during the Civil War. His letters and speeches stirred people of the Northern states to fight. His "Gettysburg Address" is one of the most famous speeches ever made. It is very short. When he gave the speech, it took only about three minutes. (*See* **Lincoln, Abraham.**)

Another president, Theodore Roosevelt, wrote many books. He wrote about government and history. He also wrote about his experiences in the "Wild West" and Africa. For a time, he made his living as a writer. (*See* **Roosevelt, Theodore.**)

There are many other famous writers from America and other parts of the world. To learn more about writing and literature, see **children's books; English writers; literature;** and **poetry.** For information on other American writers, see **Alcott, Louisa May; Hughes, Langston; White, E.B.;** and **Wilder, Laura Ingalls.**

Writers of speeches and essays (top to bottom): Patrick Henry, Abraham Lincoln, and Henry David Thoreau.

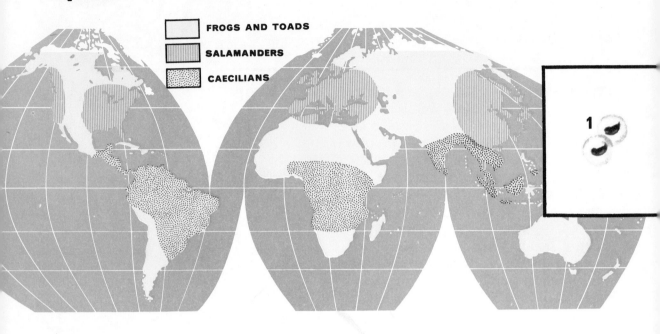

FROGS AND TOADS

SALAMANDERS

CAECILIANS

1

amphibian

Frogs, toads, and salamanders belong to a group of animals called amphibians. This name means "double life." Most amphibians spend the first part of their lives in water. They spend some or all of the adult part of their lives on land.

Amphibians are vertebrates. This means they have backbones, as do fish, reptiles, birds, and mammals. Sometimes people confuse amphibians and reptiles. An amphibian has soft, moist skin; a reptile has dry, scaly skin. Amphibian eggs do not have shells; reptile eggs have tough, leathery shells.

Amphibians are cold-blooded. Their body temperature changes with the temperature around them. They cannot stand very high or very low temperatures. Amphibians that live in hot places stay in the shade or hide underground during the hottest part of the day. Those that live in places with cold winters *hibernate*. During cold weather, they find a place where the temperature stays above freezing and go into a kind of deep sleep. Most of their body functions slow down or stop altogether. Some amphibians hibernate in the muddy bottom of a lake or

pond. Others hibernate under logs or piles of leaves.

The Amazing Amphibian Skin The most interesting part of an amphibian's body is its skin. The skin can produce two important liquids. One kind is a watery liquid called *mucus*. Mucus keeps the skin moist and makes an amphibian feel slippery. Some amphibians also produce strong poisons in their skin. Many amphibians that are very poisonous are also brightly colored. Their color warns other animals that they might be dangerous.

An amphibian's skin can be used for *respiration*—taking in oxygen and giving off carbon dioxide and other wastes, just like your lungs. Being able to "breathe" through its skin allows an amphibian to stay underwater for a long time. It also makes it possible for the animal to hibernate in the bottom of a pond.

Amphibians do not drink water. They take in water through their skins. The skin soaks up water from ponds, rivers, and even moist ground or dew-covered plants.

Kinds of Amphibians There are about 3,000 different kinds of amphibians. These animals are found all over the world, but

68

Amphibians hatch from eggs laid in the water (1). At first, they look almost like fish (2 and 3). But then they grow legs and lose their fishlike tails (4 and 5). As adults, they spend much of their time out of the water.

only in wet places. They live in lakes, ponds, rivers, and swamps. They also live on damp forest floors and in people's gardens. But they are never found in oceans or other bodies of salt water.

Amphibians can be divided into three groups. Frogs and toads form one group. They have tails when they are young, but they lose the tails as they become adults. Salamanders and newts form a second group. These amphibians have tails all their lives. The third group of amphibians are the caecilians. They live in South America and southern Asia. Caecilians have long, thin bodies and no legs. In fact, they look like worms. They spend most of their lives underground. One kind of caecilian lives in water and is a good swimmer. It looks like an eel.

The Life of Amphibians   There are three stages in an amphibian's life: egg, larva, and adult. The eggs are always laid in water and covered with a thick, jellylike coating. This protects the eggs against drying out. Amphibians lay many eggs. Some frogs lay 20,000 eggs at one time. Only a few of these eggs ever hatch. Many are eaten by fish and large insects.

The eggs that are not eaten hatch into lar-

vae. The larvae of frogs and toads are often called *tadpoles* or *polliwogs*. Amphibian larvae live in water. They have fishlike bodies and no legs. Some even have fins!

The larvae of frogs and toads feed mainly on tiny water plants and on bits of dead animals. The larvae of newts and salamanders eat mostly insects.

Like fish, amphibian larvae breathe by means of gills. To change to adults, the larvae must develop lungs so that they can breathe air. Most amphibian larvae must also grow legs. Many other changes must take place in their bodies. Tadpoles lose their gills as they change into adults. Most salamanders and newts develop lungs but do not lose their gills. But some adult salamanders have no lungs—and no gills, either. They breathe entirely through their skins.

Adult amphibians are carnivores—meat-eaters. They eat worms, crabs, and even small fish, but they feed mainly on insects, including mosquitoes and other insects that are harmful to people. In turn, many amphibians are eaten by snakes, turtles, birds, and other animals.

See also **frogs and toads; salamanders and newts;** and **animals, prehistoric.**

amplifier

A plucked guitar string is not very loud. Yet rock guitarists make very loud music. They do this by using an amplifier. An amplifier is an electrical device that can make soft sounds much louder.

We use amplifiers in many ways. When you speak into a microphone, an amplifier makes the sound of your voice much louder. In a record player, an amplifier takes a weak sound signal from the record and makes it loud enough to hear. Radio and television amplifiers do the same thing.

All amplifiers work the same way. First, a microphone or some other device must translate sound into an electrical signal. The amplifier makes the electrical signal much stronger. This amplified signal then travels to a speaker. The speaker translates the strong electrical signal back into sound.

Most amplifiers have many controls. One control lets you turn the loudness—the volume—up or down. Other controls let you decide how much low sound (bass) and high sound (treble) you want. A good amplifier can make sounds louder without changing them in any other way. A guitar will still sound like a guitar. Or, if you wish, the amplifier can change the guitar sound into something new and different.

See also **sound.**

Amundsen, Roald

Roald Amundsen explored the icy lands around both the North Pole and the South Pole. He was born in Norway in 1872. When still a young man, he began preparing for his career. He achieved a great deal because he had a strong will and made careful plans.

Amundsen became famous as commander of the first ship to sail through the Northwest Passage. Explorers had been looking for this water route between the Atlantic and Pacific oceans for nearly 400 years. It took Amundsen and his crew three years—from 1903 to 1906—to make the dangerous jour-

ney from Alaska to eastern Canada in their ship, the *Gjöa.* (*See* **Northwest Passage.**)

Amundsen was about to travel in search of the North Pole when he heard that an American explorer, Robert Peary, had gotten there first. Instead, Amundsen set out for the South Pole. In October 1911, he and four other men set out across Antarctica by dogsled. They reached the South Pole in December and set up a Norwegian flag there. (*See* **South Pole.**)

Later, Amundsen explored by air. In 1926, he flew over the North Pole in a dirigible—a balloonlike flying machine. Two years later, the explorer who had been pilot of Amundsen's dirigible disappeared in the Arctic. Amundsen set out by plane to look for him. Though the dirigible pilot was later found, Amundsen's plane was never seen again.

anatomy, *see* human body

Andersen, Hans Christian

Hans Christian Andersen was a famous writer of fairy tales. He was born in Denmark in 1805, the only child of a shoemaker and his wife. When Hans was only 11, his father died. Hans went to work in a factory to support himself and his mother. People in the factory made fun of him because he was often daydreaming instead of paying attention to his job.

When he was 14, Hans went to Copenhagen, the biggest city in Denmark. There he worked in a theater as a stagehand and singer. Then he got a scholarship that allowed him to go back to school. Afterward, Hans began to write poems, plays, and his famous fairy tales. He kept on writing until he died, at age 70, in 1875.

Andersen wrote 168 fairy tales in all, including "The Little Mermaid" and "The Princess and the Pea." Perhaps the most popular was "The Emperor's New Clothes," about an emperor who is tricked into wearing clothes made of invisible cloth.

Hans Christian Andersen (top) wrote
"The Emperor's New Clothes" (bottom).

In many ways, Andersen's life was like his popular story "The Ugly Duckling." Both Andersen and the duckling were made fun of when they were young. Yet the duckling grew up to be a swan, and Andersen grew into a man who was admired not only in Denmark but all over the world.

See also **children's books** and **fairy tale.**

Andes

The Andes, the longest mountain chain in the world, stretch for 4,500 miles (7,200 kilometers) along the west coast of South America. These mountains cover parts of Venezuela, Colombia, Ecuador, Peru, Bolivia,

Chile, and Argentina. Some peaks in the Andes are active volcanoes.

The Andes are higher than every mountain chain except the Himalaya Mountains in Asia. The Andes are so high that even the peaks near the equator have glaciers on them. The highest peak is Mount Aconcagua, in central Argentina. It is 22,834 feet (6,960 meters) above sea level. Aconcagua is the highest mountain in the Americas.

Lake Titicaca is the world's highest lake large enough for ships. It is in the northern Andes on the Peru-Bolivia border. Its surface is more than 12,000 feet (3,660 meters) above sea level, and it is more than 100 miles (160 kilometers) long.

The name *Andes* comes from an Indian word meaning "copper." Copper and other metals are mined in the Andes. In the valleys

and on the lower slopes of the mountains, there are many farms. Coffee is an important crop in the northern Andes.

Many of the people who live in the Andes are descendants of the ancient Inca, people who built a great empire in the Americas before the time of Columbus. (*See* **Inca.**)

Andorra, *see* Europe

anesthetic

An anesthetic is a drug that prevents you from feeling pain. Sometimes the dentist may give you a shot before working on a tooth. The shot makes part of your mouth numb so that the dentist can use the drill without causing pain.

The anesthetics that make only a part of you numb are called *local anesthetics.* Doctors sometimes give a local anesthetic to a patient before an operation. The patient stays awake during the operation and can follow instructions, but he or she does not feel any pain.

A *general anesthetic,* on the other hand, seems to put you completely to sleep before an operation. You feel no pain, and later you remember nothing about the operation. A general anesthetic actually makes you unconscious. If you were really only asleep, the pain of the operation would wake you up.

Anesthetics were first used in the 1840s. Before that, even having a tooth pulled was very painful. Patients were often held down by several men while the doctor operated. Sometimes, patients were given a bullet or a coin to bite down on when the pain got worse. By preventing pain, anesthetics have made important kinds of treatment possible.

See also **drugs and medicines.**

angle, *see* geometry

Anglo-Saxons

Beginning in the 400s—about 1,500 years ago—three tribes from present-day Germany and Denmark came to Britain. They were the Angles, the Saxons, and the Jutes. A British king named Vortigern had asked them to help him fight his enemies.

The three tribes came to be known as the Anglo-Saxons. They were good warriors and soon ruled the southern part of Britain themselves. The region became known as Angle-land, or (as we now spell it) England.

The Anglo-Saxons all had similar customs but did not unite under one ruler. Instead, they formed small kingdoms and often fought each other for land and power. Even after becoming Christian during the 500s and 600s, they continued to quarrel. Danish invaders took more and more of their land. In the late 800s, the kingdoms were finally united by Alfred the Great. He then defeated the Danes and brought peace to England.

After Alfred died, the Danes again fought the Anglo-Saxons. In 1066, the Normans— a people who lived in present-day France —invaded England. Led by William the Conqueror, they defeated the English. The French-speaking Normans ruled England for over 200 years.

The language of the Anglo-Saxons is called Old English. It is very different from the English we speak today. But thousands of words that we use every day come from Old English.

See also **English history** and **English language.**

Angola, *see* Africa

animal

Animals come in many sizes, shapes, and colors. Fleas and foxes are animals. So are cows and clams, butterflies and barnacles, worms and whales, penguins and people. All together, there are more than 1 million kinds of living animals.

Animals can move—they fly, climb, hop, swim, walk, and run. The cheetah (below) is the fastest runner.

Animal or Plant? Sometimes, it is difficult to tell if a living thing is an animal or a plant. A lion is clearly an animal. A dandelion is clearly a plant. But sponges and coral are also animals, even though they look something like plants. They do not *look* like lions, birds, or fish. But they *are* like lions, birds, and fish in important ways.

Most plants can make their own food. They use a green substance called *chlorophyll*. Dandelions and other plants use chlorophyll to make food. Animal cells do not contain chlorophyll, and animals cannot make their own food. Animals must get food by eating it. Some eat plants. Others, such as lions, eat other animals.

Plants cannot move from one place to another by themselves. A dandelion stays where the seed from which it grew was planted. Animals are able to move from one place to another, at least during some part of their lives. Lions move over great distances, walking and running on their four legs. They even climb trees!

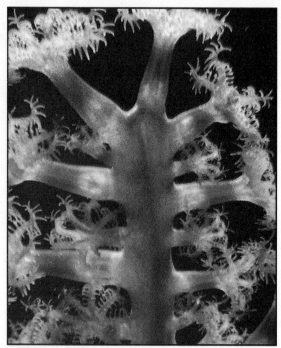

This coral looks like an underwater plant, but it is really an animal.

All plants and animals are made up of cells. Plant cells are surrounded by walls, and many plant cells look like little boxes. They have a regular shape. Animal cells do not have walls. Animal cells come in many different shapes. Some cells are round, some have long, thin branches, and some even change their shapes.

A particular kind of animal has a definite shape. For example, a lion always has one head, two eyes, four legs, a tail, one stomach, and so on. The sizes and shapes of plants are not as definite. For example, one dandelion plant may have one flower and five leaves. Another may have three flowers and ten leaves—or any number of leaves from four to twenty.

Animals need salt. Without enough salt in its body, a lion will die. The opposite is true for plants. Pouring salt water on a dandelion will kill it. Salt is poisonous to most plants.

In general, animals react quickly to things that happen around them. Plants react slowly. If you shine a bright light at a lion, the pupils of its eyes will get smaller, and the lion will quickly turn away. A dandelion will react to light, too. It will turn its leaves toward the light. But this movement will take hours or even a day or more.

Classifying Animals Scientists *classify* animals—sort them into groups. Classifying animals is much like classifying food in a supermarket, where similar kinds of foods are put together. All the kinds of bread are arranged in one place. Soft drinks are arranged in another place, meats in another, fruits in still another. Likewise, animals that are similar to one another are classified in the same group.

We have divided animals into two main groups, called *vertebrates* and *invertebrates.* Vertebrates are animals that have a backbone. Invertebrates are animals that do not have a backbone.

Move your hand up and down the middle of your back. You can feel your backbone. A backbone is a long column of small bones called *vertebrae.* Attached to the vertebrae are other bones, such as rib bones, arm bones, and leg bones. Many muscles are attached to the backbone. The backbone supports the body and makes it possible to move the body in many ways.

Many of the animals that are most familiar to us are vertebrates. They include all fish, amphibians, reptiles, birds, and mammals. Human beings are mammals and vertebrates. (*See* **amphibian; bird; fish; mammal;** and **reptile.**)

All other animals are invertebrates. The invertebrates include the following groups:

Porifera, or "pore-bearers." These are the sponges. Sponges are the simplest animals. Their bodies are shaped like sacks, with many tiny openings, called *pores.* The pores connect the inside of the sponge's body with the outside.

Coelenterates, or "animals with hollow intestines." Jellyfish, corals, and sea anemones are coelenterates. So is the Portuguese man-of-war. These ocean animals have tentacles and stinging cells.

Platyhelminths, or "flatworms." These worms have soft, flat bodies that are usually all in one piece instead of divided up into parts, called *segments*. They include planaria and flukes.

Nematodes, or "roundworms." These include tapeworms and other pests than can cause illness in animals and humans.

Annelids, or "ringed animals." Annelids are slender worms. They have segmented bodies. Earthworms, sandworms, and leeches are annelids.

Biologists divide animals into 38 *phyla*—giant families. Nine important ones are shown below.

Echinoderms, or "spiny-skinned animals." This group includes starfish, sea urchins, sand dollars, and sea cucumbers, all found in the ocean. Echinoderms usually have five arms. They also have hundreds of tiny tubelike "feet" that help them move.

Mollusks, or "soft-bodied animals." Oysters, clams, scallops, snails, slugs, squid, and octopuses are mollusks. A mollusk's soft body is enclosed in a fold of tissue called the *mantle*. Outside the mantle, there usually is a hard shell.

Arthropods, or "joint-footed animals." The body of an arthropod is divided into segments. The legs and other movable parts are jointed. The body is usually covered by a hard outer skeleton, which must be shed as the animal grows. There are six classes of arthropods. The crustaceans make up one class. Crabs, lobsters, shrimp, and barnacles are crustaceans. The spiders, scorpions, centipedes, millipedes, and insects make up the other five classes of arthropods. Insects are the largest class of animals. There are more kinds of insects on Earth than all other kinds of animals combined.

See the Index for a full list of entries on animals and animal families.

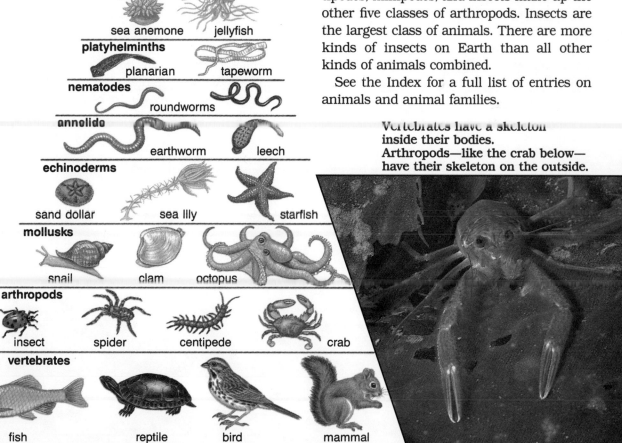

Vertebrates have a skeleton inside their bodies.
Arthropods—like the crab below—have their skeleton on the outside.

Animal Sizes Some animals are taller than a house. Others are so tiny that they can be seen only with a magnifying glass.

The largest animals are the blue whales. These giants of the sea may be 30 meters (100 feet) long—longer than a basketball court. They may weigh more than 100 tons—more than 1,500 average-size human adults!

The largest animal that lives on land is the African elephant. It may be 4 meters (13 feet) tall. Millions of years ago, animals that were even bigger walked on land—the dinosaurs. The biggest dinosaurs were 6 meters (20 feet) tall and more than 25 meters (85 feet) long.

Condors are among the largest flying birds. But the albatross has the largest wingspan. From the tip of one wing to the outstretched tip of the other wing, an albatross may measure 3.5 meters (11 feet).

Other huge animals live in the ocean. With its arms outstretched, a giant squid may be more than 15 meters (50 feet) long. The giant jellyfish may weigh almost a ton. Its body may be 2.5 meters (8 feet) wide, and its tentacles may be more than 50 meters (165 feet) long.

At the other end of the scale are the tiny animals. Many insects are very, very small. Some wasplike insects are only 0.2 millimeters (1/125 inch) long—hardly as big as a tiny grain of sand. But these little creatures have all the same parts found on much larger insects, including four wings, six legs, eyes, and a brain.

This tiny Cuban bee hummingbird is shown in its actual size.

Shrews are the smallest mammals. The pygmy shrew, which looks like a tiny baby mouse, weighs less than a dime. The smallest bird is the Cuban bee hummingbird. It is only 5 centimeters (2 inches) long.

How Animals Move Many land animals have legs. They walk, run, or jump from one place to another. Earthworms and snakes do not have legs, but they use muscles in their bodies to creep over the ground.

Some animals can fly through the air on wings. Bats can fly. So can most birds and insects.

Animals can move through the water by swimming. Whales, dolphins, fish, turtles, and frogs are excellent swimmers. Squid and jellyfish move by jet propulsion. They suck water into their bodies, then squirt it out. This shoots them forward.

Some adult animals, such as sponges, corals, and barnacles, do not move from place to place. But these animals have a different form when they are young and can swim until they take on their adult shapes.

Giant jellyfish live in the Atlantic Ocean. Their bodies can be 8 feet across, and their tentacles can reach 160 feet— the length of four houses side by side!

———160 feet———

There are animals who are hitchhikers. They travel from place to place on other animals. The remora is an ocean fish that has a sucker on top of its head. It uses the sucker to attach itself to a large fish, or to a whale or sea turtle. It eats food left over by the large animal. It does not hurt the large animal. If it cannot hitch a ride, it swims by itself through the water.

What Animals Eat People can eat many different kinds of foods. We eat both plants and animals. Therefore, we may be called *omnivores,* which means "eaters of everything." Some other animals are omnivores, too. The skunk, for example, eats fruits and grains, and it also eats insects, frogs, mice, and bird eggs. Bluebirds, raccoons, pigs, and chickens are all omnivores.

Other animals eat only plant foods. They are called *herbivores,* which means "plant-eaters." Horses are herbivores. They eat only grasses. Porcupines, bees, and cows are some of the herbivores.

Still other animals eat only meat. They are called *carnivores,* which means "meat-eaters." Lions are carnivores. They chase and kill zebras, buffalo, and other large animals. Walruses, octopuses, owls, and most lizards are some of the carnivores.

Most carnivores may also be called *predators,* because they hunt and kill living animals for food. Skunks and lions are predators, and so are centipedes, jellyfish, eagles, and killer whales. People are the major predators on Earth. We kill animals for food, clothing, and other uses.

Some omnivores and carnivores are not predators. They eat the meat of animals that have died natural deaths, or the remains of animals killed by predators. They are called *scavengers.* The vulture is a scavenger. Some animals, such as coyotes and hyenas, are both predators and scavengers. They may chase and kill an animal, or they may eat leftovers from another predator's dinner.

Some animals eat one kind of food when they are young and another kind when they are adults. Tadpoles, which are the young of frogs and toads, usually eat plants. Adult frogs and toads are carnivores. They eat insects, fish, and other animals. Young blister beetles eat other insects. Adult blister beetles feed on plants.

We call animals such as bloodsucking leeches *parasites.* Parasites live on or in other animals. They hurt their hosts—the animals they live on. Over a long period of time, they may actually kill the hosts. A leech is a kind of worm that attaches itself to a host. It makes a small cut in the host's skin and sucks up the host's blood. Other parasites include tapeworms and fish lice.

Some animals eat only a few kinds of food. Koalas eat only the leaves of eucalyptus trees. Silkworms eat only the leaves of mulberry trees. And anteaters eat only ants and termites.

Being able to eat many different foods is an important advantage. If one food is not available, the animal can eat something else. An animal that can eat foods available only at certain times of the year as well as foods available all year has a better chance of surviving because of the extra food supply. For example, the grizzly bear eats squirrels all year, when it can catch them. In spring, the grizzly also eats a lot of roots. In early summer, it also eats grasses. In late summer, it feeds mostly on berries and salmon.

This skunk is eating an egg from a bird's nest—it is a scavenger.

Where Animals Live   Animals live in every part of our planet. They are found on the highest mountains and in the deepest seas, in the icy regions near the poles and in the hot jungles on the equator, in deserts and in swamps.

No animal lives alone. It is surrounded by other living things. All the living things in an area form a large group called a *community.* The plants and animals that live in a pond, for example, are a community. No two communities are exactly alike. Frogs may be found in one pond but not in another. Water lilies may grow in one but not in another.

There are many kinds of communities. Forests, coral reefs, swamps, and deserts are all examples of communities. Small communities often exist within larger ones. The living things in the soil of a forest community make up a soil community. The living things in a rotting log on the forest floor form still another community.

A community is one group of living things. Every community is made up of even smaller groups called *populations.* Together, all the individuals of the same kind that live in the same area make up one population. For example, a pond is a community. The frogs in the pond are a population. The fish in the same pond are another population.

Each animal in a community has a particular place where it lives, called its *habitat.*

The habitat provides the animal's food and shelter. In a forest community, you may see ants, squirrels, and deer. The habitat of an ant is small. It lives in an anthill. It may never leave the anthill. A squirrel's habitat may be large. It may include the inside of a hollow tree trunk and the land around the tree trunk. The deer's habitat may be larger still. It may be the entire forest.

There are many kinds of habitats. Land habitats include grasslands, forests, and deserts. Land habitats in different parts of the world may have very different communities. The grasslands of western North America are often called *prairies.* Animals that live on the prairies include bison, deer, wolves, rabbits, and skunks. The grasslands of tropical Africa are called *savannas.* Lions, giraffes, zebras, and elephants live there.

Freshwater habitats include ponds, lakes, swamps, and rivers. Again, the many different habitats all have their own kinds of animals. Brown trout live only in cool, running water. Carp like warm, quiet ponds.

There are many *marine,* or saltwater, habitats, too. These exist at different levels of the oceans. Some fish live near the water's surface, where green plants and light can be found. Other fish live far below the ocean's surface, where it is always dark. They look very different from the fish that live near the surface. Deep-water fish have very tiny eyes.

A rotting log and the forest floor around it provide a home for many different kinds of animals.

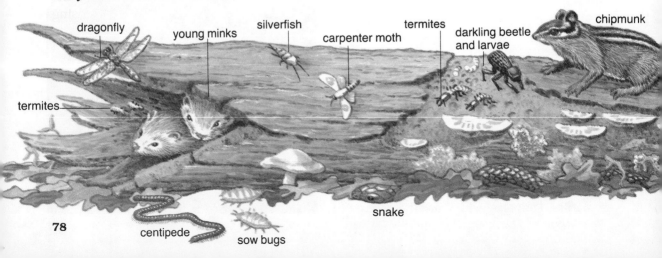

dragonfly   young minks   silverfish   carpenter moth   termites   darkling beetle and larvae   chipmunk

termites

centipede   sow bugs   snake

By selective breeding, people have helped create many sizes and shapes of dogs. Some kinds have special jobs. Collies can herd sheep, bloodhounds can track animals or people, and terriers can catch rats or mice.

They have very large mouths that are filled with daggerlike teeth.

Tidal pools form another marine habitat. Twice a day, the tides move in and out of a tidal pool. Starfish, clams, crabs, and barnacles are some of the animals that live in tidal-pool communities.

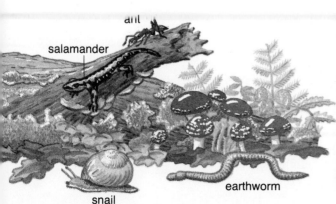

ant

salamander

snail

earthworm

animal breeding

There are many kinds of cattle. Some, known as beef cattle, are good for their meat. Others, known as dairy cattle, give lots of milk. How did all these different kinds of cattle develop? In many cases, humans have used a method called *selective breeding.* Selective breeding means carefully choosing parents to produce young. If both parents are big, healthy beef cattle, their calf should be big and healthy, too.

Farmers with herds of dairy cattle want cows that give lots of milk. The farmers can help produce such cows by deciding which two animals should mate to produce a new calf. For a mother, a farmer chooses a cow that has given lots of milk. For a father, a farmer chooses a bull whose mother and daughters have given lots of milk. A female calf born to these parents will probably be a good milk producer. Soon all the cows in a herd will be good milk producers.

Animals are not bred just for food. For hundreds of years, people have bred dogs for special traits. The different breeds of dog we know today were produced by selective breeding. Terriers, small but strong, were bred to hunt rats and burrowing animals on farms. Bloodhounds have a keen sense of smell and can track animals for hunters. Collies and German shepherds were bred to help herd sheep.

See also **heredity.**

animal communication

Animals "tell" many things about the way they feel. They communicate with one another, and with people, too. A cat purrs when it is happy. It meows when it wants food or attention. It growls or hisses when it is angry. It rubs its head against your leg to say "I love you."

Scientists have learned a lot about how wild animals communicate. For example,

Koko the gorilla can use sign language. She calls the kitten "Smokey" because of its color.

vervet monkeys have three different calls to warn one another when an enemy comes near. One call signals that a leopard is close by. Another says, "An eagle!" and a third says, "Look out for the snake!"

Animals use signals to warn other animals to stay out of their territory. Many male birds do this by singing. Their songs warn other males to stay away. Some male frogs warn other male frogs to stay away by thumping the ground with their stomachs. When a group of howler monkeys roars, it tells other monkeys, "This is our territory. Keep out!" A howler monkey's call can be heard up to 2.5 kilometers (1½ miles) away.

Animals must also communicate with one another to find a mate to have young with. A male bird may have a special mating call that tells females he is looking for a mate. A male toad calls to a female with a loud croak.

Some animals have other ways of communicating. A firefly uses flashes of light to attract a mate. A fish called the red cichlid uses color. This fish is usually brownish, with a yellow belly. It turns a brilliant red when it is ready to mate.

Animal movements may communicate messages, too. When a honeybee finds a good source of food, it returns to the hive and does a dance to tell other bees where the food is. Male hermit crabs wave their large claws to attract females. Male turkeys parade to attract females, fanning their tails wide and dragging their wings on the ground.

Animals often receive messages with their sense of smell. A male rabbit marks his territory with a special fluid made by glands on his chin. The rabbit scratches the glands with one of his back paws. This releases the fluid. Other rabbits smell it and know they are on his territory.

We can teach some animals to communicate with us. A dog can be taught to recognize its name. Some chimpanzees have learned to understand spoken English. A gorilla named Koko can use American Sign Language, a language invented to help deaf people communicate.

animal homes

Animal homes are as unlike each other as the animals are themselves. For beavers, home is a lodge built of branches out in the middle of a pond. For termites, it is an elaborate nest. For spiders, it is a delicate web. For barnacles, home is a spot on a rock.

Some homes are permanent, which means that the animals live in them all the time. Once a barnacle settles down on a rock, it cements itself in place. It spends the rest of its life in that one spot.

The chiton, a relative of snails and clams, also lives on a rock on the ocean floor. All day long, it holds on tight. At night, it leaves to look for food. Then it returns to exactly the same spot on the rock.

Other homes are temporary. A hermit crab uses an empty snail shell as a temporary home. The hermit crab's home is like a house trailer. It travels wherever the crab does. Once the crab grows too big for the shell, it moves to a larger shell.

The Carolina leaf roller makes a new home every day. At night, this insect hunts for food. Early in the morning, before the sun rises, it starts building its new home. It rolls a leaf around itself, like a blanket. Then it spins a silk thread. It takes this thread in its mouth and "sews" together the edges of the leaf. After it has closed all the openings, the leaf roller curls its antennae over its back and goes to sleep.

Animals make their homes everywhere: in the highest treetops, in caves, under rocks, on snowy mountains. Many insects, such as ants and termites, live in people's homes. Mice, too, build nests in people's homes.

Worms and many other animals live underground. Some of these animals have sharp claws on their front feet. They use their claws to dig tunnels or holes called *burrows*. Moles build long burrows in which they spend almost their whole lives. Other animals, such as rabbits and rats, spend most of the day in their burrows. In the evening, they come out to gather food.

The leaf roller (left) rolls up in a leaf to sleep.
A beaver home in a shallow pond has "doors" underwater to keep out unfriendly animals that can't swim.

These bobcats were born
in a den among the rocks.

Many animals move around almost all the time. They do not have a home that they use regularly. They stop traveling only when it is time to have young. Then they may build a nest or other home. Some kinds of fish build nests among water plants when they are ready to lay eggs. A bass makes a nest on gravel at the bottom of a stream or pond. But most fish rest wherever they happen to stop.

Bears, wolves, foxes, and many other animals live in homes called *dens* for part of the year. The den may be a cave, a pile of rocks, or a hollow log. Foxes sometimes use empty burrows or even dig their own burrows. The animals use the den only while they hibernate or raise young.

Most birds do not have a special home during much of the year. They make nests only when it is time to lay eggs and raise young. No two kinds of birds build exactly the same sort of nest. Terns make a shallow hole in the ground. Orioles build hanging nests that look like long socks. The weaverbird weaves hundreds of pieces of grass into a hollow ball. Kingfishers dig tunnels in riverbanks. Grebes build rafts in marshes. Cliff swallows make mud nests.

Bird nests vary greatly in size. Some hummingbird nests are only 2.5 centimeters (1 inch) in diameter. On the other hand, bald eagles make huge nests and may use the

same nest for many years. Each year, they add another layer to the nest. One bald eagle nest in Ohio was 2.5 meters (8½ feet) across and about 3.5 meters (12 feet) deep. It weighed about a ton.

Although birds build homes for a short time only, many birds have a home area, called a *territory*. They live, find food, sleep, and raise their young in their territory. Many other kinds of animals also have home territories that they defend. For a lizard, the home territory may be the area around a log. For a mountain lion, the home territory may cover many square miles.

Some animals, like polar bears, live alone. They join other polar bears only when it is time to mate.

Other animals live in groups. The groups may build large homes in which all the animals in the group live. A beehive is home for thousands of bees. It has many rooms and passages. A prairie-dog town is made up of many burrows. Entrances to the burrows are marked by high mounds of soil. The burrows have long tunnels. There are special rooms in which the young are raised. There is even a listening room, near the ground surface. There a prairie dog can hear what is happening above.

Some animals have a summer home and a winter home. These may be far apart. The summer home of the Canada goose is in Canada or the northern United States. In fall, most geese begin to fly south. They head for their winter homes in the southern United States, where it is warm. In spring, they return north for the summer. Some Canada geese, however, have learned to live all year in parts of New York, New Jersey, and Connecticut. (*See* **migration**.)

The desert tortoise lives in a den in the winter, then moves outdoors when the weather gets warm. Mud puppies and other salamanders may move from one part of a lake to another as the seasons change. Lobsters and crabs live near the surface of the ocean in summer. Then they move downward, to deeper water, for the winter.

animals, endangered

In the 1800s, passenger pigeons were the most common birds in North America. People shot the birds and today there are none left. They are *extinct*—they have died out. An extinct animal can never reappear.

Many *species*—kinds of animals—are in danger of becoming extinct. For example, there are few blue whales. Gorillas, giant pandas, tigers, and California condors are some other endangered species.

Extinction is not new. Dinosaurs became extinct thousands of years ago. Today, humans are the main cause of animal extinction. We have hunted and killed so many of some kinds of animals that few or none remain to produce young. This almost happened to the buffalo (the American bison). Many other animals are still threatened.

People also destroy animal habitats. We cut down forests and build houses and roads where animals lived. (*See* **animal homes.**)

Some animals are endangered because people like unusual pets. They will pay a lot of money for rare monkeys, birds, and tropical fish. Not enough of the animals remain in the wild for them to survive.

Pollution also hurts animals. Many birds are endangered because of *pesticides*—chemicals used to kill insects and other animals that humans regard as pests. The birds eat insects that have been poisoned by pesticides. The bald eagle, America's symbol, almost became extinct because of pesticides.

Many people are working hard to help endangered animals. Governments have passed laws that limit hunting. They have also set aside parks and wildlife areas for animals, and outlawed some dangerous pesticides. Many zoos have special breeding programs to help endangered animals produce young. These zoos also protect the young so that they grow up safely and can produce young themselves. (*See* **zoo.**)

Not long ago, a large water bird called the whooping crane seemed about to die out. Laws were passed to protect a marsh in Texas where whooping cranes spend the winter. The birds' summer home in Canada was also protected. Today, whooping cranes are increasing in numbers.

With help from people, other endangered animals may also survive.

The giant panda (left) is an endangered animal. The great auk (above) is extinct. It was hunted to death by humans in the 1800s.

animals, prehistoric

Millions of years ago, strange kinds of animals lived on Earth. Dinosaurs were some of the biggest, but there were many other kinds of animals, too. Many of these animals disappeared before there were people to see them. They are called *prehistoric animals* because they lived before the history of human beings began.

Until the late 1700s, people did not know about prehistoric animals. Then they began finding clues called *fossils*. Fossils are the remains of living things preserved in rock, amber, ice, or other long-lasting materials. The hard parts of an animal—teeth, shells, and bones—make good fossils. The soft parts usually do not. (*See* **fossil.**)

A French scientist, Georges Cuvier, was one of the first to realize that fossils are the remains of ancient living things. In 1796, he found the bones of giant sloths in South America. Sloths are slow-moving, furry animals. The bones that Cuvier found were much bigger than those of any sloth alive today. Cuvier showed that prehistoric sloths

Georges Cuvier identified fossils of the giant sloth in 1796.

could stand on the ground and feed on the lower branches of avocado trees. He also found the bones of giant lizardlike creatures that could fly. He convinced many scientists that there really had been prehistoric animals. Soon, other scientists were finding fossils of prehistoric creatures.

Invertebrates The very first animals lived in the seas, at least 1,300 million years ago. We call them *invertebrates,* because they did not have backbones. Many of them had no hard parts at all, and so they did not leave many fossils. For this reason, we don't know much about them.

Gradually, many different kinds of invertebrates developed. By 600 million years ago, there were sponges, jellyfish, worms, and animals with shells.

One family of animals with shells were called *brachiopods*. Their hard shells looked like clamshells. They are sometimes called *lampshells*, because they have the same shape as ancient Roman lamps. Many were about 2.5 centimeters (1 inch) across. Over the ages, more than 25,000 different kinds of brachiopods have existed. A few kinds are still alive today.

The sea lilies were members of another ancient group. Though they looked like flowers, sea lilies were animals related to jellyfish. Most sea lilies lived attached to the ocean floor. On their heads were long arms that waved back and forth in the water, like petals. The sea lily's body was often long and slender, like a plant stem. Some sea lilies still exist. They look much like their ancestors did hundreds of millions of years ago.

Some of the most interesting invertebrates of long ago were *arthropods*—animals with hard shells and jointed legs. Insects, crabs, spiders, and centipedes are examples of arthropods that are alive today.

The trilobite was an important early arthropod. Trilobites appeared about 550 million years ago and were among the most common animals on Earth for more than 300 million years. Most early trilobites were less than 10 centimeters (4 inches) long. We

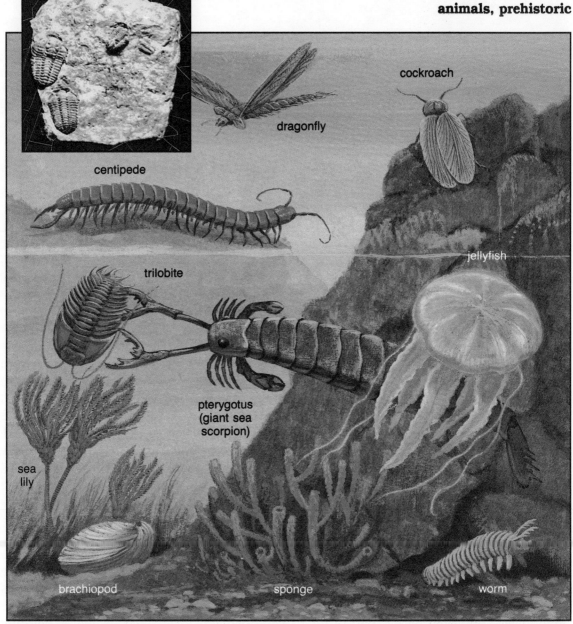

centipede

dragonfly

cockroach

trilobite

jellyfish

pterygotus
(giant sea
scorpion)

sea
lily

brachiopod

sponge

worm

Some of these animals lived on Earth for millions of years. Above is a trilobite fossil.
These small insectlike creatures were once the most important animals on Earth.

know that more than 10,000 different kinds of trilobites existed. Now there are none. They are extinct.

Sea scorpions formed another early group of arthropods. The *Pterygotus* sea scorpion could be longer than 2 meters (6 feet). This powerful swimmer had one pair of legs shaped like paddles and a smaller pair of legs for catching and holding prey. Pterygotus was a terror of the sea, attacking and eating fish and other animals.

Ammonites, which belonged to a group

called *cephalopods,* appeared about 225 million years ago. They looked something like squid and lived inside coiled, chambered shells. Different kinds of ammonites lived in different kinds of shells. There were ammonites on Earth for more than 300 million years. Eventually, they died out, too.

The first animals to live entirely on land were arthropods. Some arthropods were huge. *Arthropleura* grew almost 2 meters (6 feet) long, as big as some people! It did not have many enemies.

The earliest insects developed more than 400 million years ago. They crawled along the ground because they had no wings. Insects developed wings about 40 million years later. Some of these prehistoric insects were very large. One giant dragonfly had a wingspan of 72 centimeters (28 inches).

Vertebrates   Animals with backbones are called *vertebrates*. The earliest animals with backbones were fish. A fish has a backbone from head to tail. Most of the bones in the fish's body are attached to this backbone.

The first fish appeared about 450 million years ago. Their bodies were covered with heavy armor to protect them from sea scorpions, and they did not have jaws. These fish lived on the ocean floor. They sucked up mud from the bottom and strained food out of it. Some fish still eat this way.

Placoderms were the first fish with jaws. Like earlier fish, they had bodies covered with armor. The first placoderms were small. Later, they grew larger and one kind was almost 10 meters (30 feet) long. A person could have stood in its open mouth!

Coelacanths are fish with thick, fleshy body parts called *lobes*. Scientists thought that coelacanths became extinct about 65 million years ago. Then, in 1938, one was caught off the coast of South Africa. It was almost exactly like the ancient coelacanths. Since then, others have been found.

The first vertebrates to live on land were amphibians—animals that live part of their lives in water and part on land. Scientists believe they developed from a kind of fish that could use its fins to crawl on land. The first

This marbled salamander may be a relative of Ichthyostega on the next page.

amphibians appeared about 350 million years ago.

The first true amphibian we know of—*Ichthyostega*—was also the first animal to have ears. It was about 1 meter (3 feet) long, and like a fish in some ways, but it had real legs for crawling on land. Many different kinds of amphibians developed later. Amphibians that are alive today include frogs, toads, and salamanders. (*See* **amphibian.**)

Reptiles are animals with backbones and scaly bodies. The first reptile was small and looked like a lizard. It lived about 300 million years ago. Later, there were many kinds of reptiles. They lived on land and in water. Some could even fly!

Some reptiles were huge. There were turtles as long as 3.5 meters (12 feet) and crocodiles 15 meters (50 feet) long. Dinosaurs, the largest animals ever to walk on the earth, were reptiles. One kind of dinosaur was 24 meters (80 feet) long. (*See* **dinosaur.**)

Mesosaurs were ancient reptiles that lived in the sea. They were slim animals about a foot long and looked something like a lizard. The mesosaur had webbed feet, a long neck and tail, and lots of sharp, tiny teeth that it used to catch and hold fish.

Ichthyosaurs were reptiles that looked like fish. They had streamlined bodies and fish-like tails. Plesiosaurs were sea reptiles that looked more like dinosaurs. Some had long necks and small heads. Their arms and legs were shaped like paddles. Some plesiosaurs were more than 10 meters (40 feet) long.

Pterosaurs—the "flying lizards" discovered by Cuvier—were prehistoric reptiles that could fly. Thin flaps of skin stretching from their front legs to their back legs served as wings. Pterosaurs could glide for long distances, but they were not very good fliers. They could not flap their wings very well. Some pterosaurs were as small as sparrows. Others were giants. One had a wingspan of more than 9 meters (30 feet). It was the largest animal ever to fly. (*See* **reptile.**)

Birds and mammals are two other kinds of vertebrates. An early bird, *Archaeopteryx*,

lived about 140 million years ago. It was about the size of a crow, and had wings and feathers like birds of today. Unlike any bird we know today, however, it also had teeth, claws on its wings, and a tail like a lizard's. (*See* **birds of the past.**)

The first mammals appeared about 200 million years ago. They were the size of mice and probably ate small animals, worms, insects—and maybe dinosaur eggs. (*See* **mammals of the past.**)

The last dinosaurs died about 65 million years ago. After that, mammals became the most powerful form of life, even though no land mammals grew as large as the largest dinosaurs. The largest land mammal of all time was a hornless rhinoceros that stood 6 meters (18 feet) high—taller than today's giraffe.

pterosaur

We can tell what prehistoric animals looked like from their fossil bones. Most of the earliest animals lived in the water.

ichthyostega

ichthyosaur

mesosaur

coelacanth

placoderm

ammonite

plesiosaur

On America's 200th anniversary in 1976, many towns and cities held parades.

anniversary

An anniversary is a day for remembering some important event in the past. People usually celebrate an anniversary on the same day of the year that the event took place.

A birthday is one kind of anniversary. It celebrates the day a person was born. Some birthdays are especially important. For example, at age 16 in many states, a person is old enough to drive. At 18, young adults gain the right to vote.

Many families celebrate wedding anniversaries. Two special wedding anniversaries are the 25th and the 50th. It is a custom to give the married couple gifts made of silver on their 25th anniversary, and gifts made of gold on their 50th. These celebrations are called the *silver anniversary* and the *golden anniversary*.

Many religious holidays are anniversaries. For example, the Jewish holiday of Passover celebrates the freeing of the Jews from slavery in ancient Egypt. The Christian holiday of Christmas celebrates the birth of Jesus.

Most countries also celebrate the anniversaries of important events in their histories. In the United States, the Fourth of July is sometimes called Independence Day. It is the anniversary of the day in 1776 when the United States declared its independence from Great Britain. In France, the most important national holiday is Bastille Day, celebrated on July 14. On July 14, 1789, the people of Paris rose against their king and stormed a prison named the Bastille, beginning the French Revolution.

Other anniversaries include the birthdays of great men and women. For example, Americans celebrate the anniversaries of the birth of George Washington, Abraham Lincoln, and Martin Luther King, Jr., every year.

Often, there are special celebrations on the 100th anniversary—the centennial—of an important event. In 1876, the United States held a great world's fair to mark the centennial of the Declaration of Independence. In 1976, for the 200th anniversary—the bicentennial—there were special celebrations in many cities and towns. In 1992, the peoples of North and South America celebrate the 500th anniversary—the quincentennial—of Columbus's discovery of America.

ant

Ants are the world's most common insects. We know of some 3,500 kinds of ants. Ants are found in forests, deserts, and gardens, everywhere from the tropics to the Arctic.

An ant is easy to recognize. It has six legs and three main body parts. The second and third parts are separated by a narrow "waist." On its head are a pair of long feelers, called *antennae*. The ant uses its antennae to touch, taste, and smell the things around it. Ants communicate partly by stroking other ants with their own antennae.

Many ants are "armed" at both ends. All ants can bite with *pincers*—tiny, clawlike body parts—near their mouths, and most have stingers at the rear. Some ants give off an awful-smelling substance when attacked.

During its life, an ant passes through four very different stages: egg, larva, pupa, and adult. The eggs are white and very tiny. The larvae that hatch from the eggs are small, white, and legless, something like tiny worms. After the larvae eat and grow fat, they enter the pupal stage. During this stage, they change into adults.

Ants live in groups called *colonies.* Some kinds form small colonies with only a few individuals. Others form huge colonies of as many as 100,000 ants.

Each colony has at least one queen. A queen's job is to lay eggs. Most of the eggs develop into workers. Workers are females that do not have wings and cannot reproduce. The workers are always busy, taking care of the larvae, gathering food, and defending the colony.

The rest of the queen's eggs develop into males or *fertile* females—females that can mate and lay eggs. Males and fertile females (the future queens) have wings. Once they become adults, they fly away from the nest and mate. The males die soon after the mating flight. The females form new colonies.

Most ant colonies live in nests. Underground nests complete with rooms and long tunnels are the most common kind. Ants also make nests in stems, in nuts, and in other parts of plants. Still others dig a maze of tunnels in logs.

Some kinds of ants do not make nests. Certain kinds of army ants, for example, are always on the move. They travel in long columns, eating any animal in their path. At night, they may rest in a hollow log or other sheltered spot.

Ants such as army ants are *carnivorous*—they eat other animals. Other kinds of ants eat only plant matter. Still others have a purely liquid diet, feeding on nectar from flowers or on honeydew made by *aphids*—tiny, plant-eating insects. Some kinds of ants even keep herds of aphids the way we keep dairy cows.

See also **insect.**

In underground nests, ants grow food (left) or store food (center).
They also make rooms (right) for the queen, for eggs to hatch, and for larvae to grow.

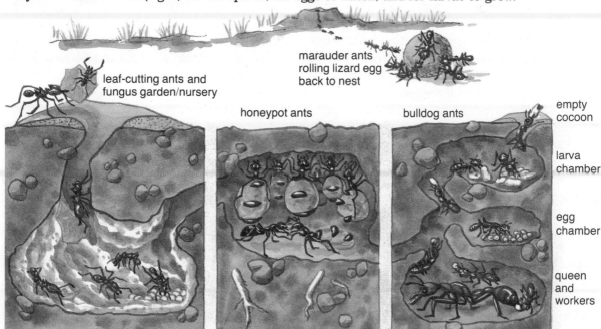

leaf-cutting ants and fungus garden/nursery

marauder ants rolling lizard egg back to nest

honeypot ants

bulldog ants

empty cocoon

larva chamber

egg chamber

queen and workers

Antarctica

Antarctica is the icy continent at "the bottom of the world." This is where the South Pole is located.

Antarctica is the coldest place on Earth. The average temperature is below 0° F (below −18° C). In 1983, at a Soviet research base called Vostok, the temperature fell to −128.9° F (−89.4° C), the coldest temperature ever recorded on the earth's surface.

An automatic weather station records the freezing Antarctic temperatures.

Antarctica's penguins cannot fly, but are skilled swimmers.

The cold makes Antarctica one of the strangest places on Earth. It is one and one-half times the size of the United States, but there are no ordinary towns, no farms, and no factories. There are no ordinary trees or flowers, and no large land animals.

Most of the land of Antarctica has never been seen by people because it is under thousands of feet of ice. Ninety percent of all the ice in the world is here. Some of it is more than 2½ miles (4 kilometers) deep. The ice contains more fresh water than every lake and river in the world combined. Only the sides of some mountains are not covered by ice or snow.

Land Antarctica is shaped something like a mushroom. The high Transantarctic Mountains cross the continent, separating the cap of the mushroom from the stem. The cap is East Antarctica, a giant, ice-covered

plateau more than 2,500 miles across. If you traveled north from here, you would reach Africa, Australia, or Asia.

West Antarctica, the stem of the mushroom, is much smaller than East Antarctica. It has the continent's highest mountains. If you were to travel north from here, you would reach South America, the western coast of the United States, or islands in the Pacific Ocean.

A giant inlet or bay, called a sea, lies on each side of West Antarctica. The Ross Sea faces the South Pacific Ocean and contains the Ross Ice Shelf, the largest body of floating ice in the world. It is about as large as Texas. The United States has a research station and airfield at McMurdo Sound, on the Ross Ice Shelf.

The Weddell Sea is the bay that faces the South Atlantic. From one edge of this bay, a long finger of mountainous land called the Antarctic Peninsula stretches to within 600 miles of South America.

Plants and Animals The water around the continent, often called the Antarctic Ocean, is really made up of the southern parts of the Atlantic, Pacific, and Indian oceans. Most of it freezes over during the winter. A shifting ice pack stretches north from the coast for hundreds of miles. This icy ocean is home to most of Antarctica's animal life. Whales and many kinds of seals spend their lives near the Antarctic coast.

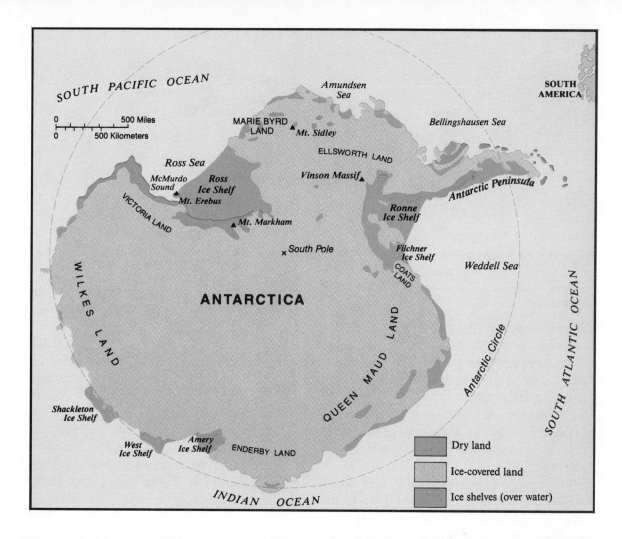

Millions of penguins live along the edges of the great ice shelves. Many kinds of birds visit the Antarctic during the summer.

On the Antarctic Peninsula and in places where some mountain peaks are free of ice, simple plants such as lichens, mosses, and a few grasses grow during the short summer. On the rest of the continent, nothing large enough to see without a microscope survives the fierce winter.

Exploration Antarctica was the last continent to be discovered. The first person to search for it was Captain James Cook. This great English explorer sailed all around the continent in 1772. But the ice was so thick that he could not get his wooden ship close enough to see land. A few other explorers sailed close to Antarctica in the 1800s, but could not get close enough to go ashore.

Early in the 1900s, two groups of daring explorers finally camped on Antarctica. Each hoped to be the first to reach the South Pole, near the middle of the continent. Roald Amundsen, a Norwegian, reached it first. He and four others arrived at the South Pole on December 14, 1911, after traveling nearly eight weeks by dogsled. The next month, Robert F. Scott, from Britain, reached the Pole. He and his men had traveled by pony, but the ponies died. On the way back, Scott and all his men died of starvation and cold. (*See* **Amundsen, Roald** and **Scott, Robert.**)

Soon, airplanes were being used to explore the continent. In 1928, U.S. Navy Commander Richard E. Byrd was the first to fly over the South Pole. In 1957 and 1958, many countries set up research stations in Antarctica. They signed a treaty saying that Antarctica can be used only for peaceful purposes. No country may build military bases in Antarctica.

See also **South Pole.**

Anteaters have long snouts for reaching into ant tunnels.

anteater

The anteater is an unusual animal that lives in forests and grasslands in Central and South America. It eats ants and termites. A large anteater may eat 30,000 ants and termites in a single day.

An anteater has strong legs and long, curved claws. It has a long, slender snout, and a tiny mouth with no teeth but a very long tongue.

The anteater uses its claws to tear apart anthills and termite nests. Then it pokes its sticky tongue into the ant tunnels. The ants or termites get stuck, and the anteater eats them. The anteater may push its tongue in and out of an anthill as many as 160 times a minute!

There are three kinds of anteaters. The largest is the giant anteater. It is about the size of a German shepherd dog. Giant anteaters live on the ground. The collared anteater, tamandua, is about half the size of the giant anteater. It lives on the ground and in trees. The pygmy anteater is about the size of a squirrel and lives only in trees. It eats termites that build nests high in the treetops.

See also mammal.

antelope, *see* deer and antelope

Anthony, Susan B.

Susan B. Anthony was an American who fought for women's rights, especially for *woman suffrage*—women's right to vote in public elections. She was called "the woman who changed the mind of a nation."

When Anthony was born, in Massachusetts in 1820, most people believed that all women should be wives and mothers and stay at home. Women could not vote in elections. They usually could not own their own land or study in high schools or colleges. Susan's family believed that both men and women should fight for a better world. They encouraged her to speak out against black slavery and against the use of alcohol.

Susan became a teacher. She tried to join the *temperance* movement, which was against making or selling beer, wine, and liquor. But she was not allowed to speak

Susan B. Anthony was a pioneer in the fight for women's rights.

at meetings because she was a woman. She decided to fight for women's rights.

In 1869, Anthony and her friend Elizabeth Cady Stanton started the National Woman Suffrage Association. In 1872, Anthony tried to vote in the presidential election. She was arrested and fined $100. Though many people made fun of her, she kept forming ever-larger suffrage groups.

When Susan B. Anthony died, in 1906, women still were not allowed to vote. Finally, in 1920, the United States changed its laws and allowed women to vote in all elections. In 1979, the U.S. government issued a new one-dollar coin with Susan B. Anthony's picture on it. She was the first woman to appear on a U.S. coin.

See also **women's rights.**

anthropology

Anthropology is the scientific study of people and their ways of life. The name *anthropology* comes from Greek words that mean "the study of human beings." Anthropologists —experts in anthropology—ask questions like these: How long ago did the earliest humans live? What differences are there among groups of people today? Do all peoples have some religious beliefs?

Anthropologists answer these questions by doing different kinds of research. Some look for the bones and other remains of people who lived thousands of years ago. Others go to live among peoples in distant lands.

Physical Anthropology Physical anthropology is the study of people's physical size and shape. Many physical anthropologists want to know what humans looked like thousands of years ago. They search for clues in the ruins these peoples left behind.

Physical anthropology began in the 1800s, when some interesting bones were discovered in the Neanderthal Valley in Germany. They looked like human bones, but not like the bones of people today. Anthropologists finally were able to show that the Neanderthal peoples lived about 50,000 years ago.

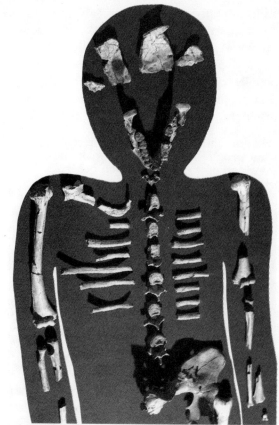

These are the fossil bones of Lucy, a humanlike creature who died about 3 million years ago. She was fully grown, but was only about 4 feet tall—the height of a third grader.

Since the 1800s, many other bones of humans and humanlike beings have been found. In the 1970s, the bones of some very ancient humanlike beings were found in Africa. One was a skeleton fossil of a young female. Scientists named her Lucy. Lucy was only 105 centimeters (3½ feet) tall. But she did walk standing up on two feet. Lucy's skeleton may be more than 3 million years old. She and others like her could be ancient ancestors of today's human beings.

Anthropologists have found remains of early humans and ancient humanlike beings in Africa, Europe, and Asia. In some places, they have also found tools that ancient peoples used for hunting and for cutting up food. The more things we find, the more we learn about these ancient peoples. There are still many mysteries, however. For example, we know very little about the kind of life Lucy and her family lived.

Some physical anthropologists study the peoples of today's world. They have found that peoples in all parts of the world are surprisingly alike. They share the same blood

Cultural anthropologists are interested in what people wear, how they work and play, and how they treat each other.

types, grow to about the same size, and use their minds in the same ways.

Cultural Anthropology   The customs, behavior, and beliefs of a community of people are called its *culture*. Cultural anthropologists are especially interested in the ways different peoples live in today's world. One way anthropologists can learn about another culture is to live among the people they are studying. Margaret Mead, a famous American anthropologist, did this. For several months, she lived on the island of Samoa in the Pacific Ocean. She was especially interested in the way young people of Samoa grew up. (*See* **Mead, Margaret.**)

Anthropologists study the many ways people meet their needs for food and shelter. Have you ever thought of eating guinea pigs? In the past, Indian groups in South America thought guinea pigs were a special treat. Some peoples in Africa enjoy eating worms and insects. On the other hand, there are

some people who won't eat some foods that we like—milk, for example.

People in different places also wear different kinds of clothing. In the United States, men wear pants and shirts. In Arab countries, most men wear long, loose robes. In some cultures, men wear only small cloths, and women wear only short skirts. How people dress depends partly on climate and partly on the customs of each culture.

All cultures raise children in some kind of family. Families are organized in many different ways, however, and they treat children differently. In some cultures, children are never punished. In others, they are severely beaten if they do something wrong. (*See* **family.**)

Every culture has some kind of government to keep order. In small communities, the older men may meet to make decisions. In larger communities, government is more complicated. In the United States, people elect leaders to run their government.

Every culture also has some kind of religion. Some people believe in one god. Others worship many. Some believe that after we die, we go to a special place above or under the earth. Others believe that the souls of the dead stay among the living as ghosts. Some peoples believe that there is a special life force not only in people and animals but also in nonliving objects, such as rocks and waterfalls.

See also **archaeology.**

antibiotic

Antibiotics are drugs given to people with certain infections or illnesses. Two well-known antibiotics are penicillin and streptomycin. There are more than 80 others.

For many years, antibiotics were thought of as miracle drugs. Before antibiotics were discovered, many people died of such diseases as scarlet fever and pneumonia. These diseases are usually caused by bacteria. Antibiotics keep bacteria from growing and reproducing. They help people get well.

Doctors also give antibiotics to people who have had operations or have been injured. The drugs help to protect them from serious infections. Antibiotics are also used to prevent infections in some animals and plants.

Alexander Fleming, a Scottish scientist, discovered antibiotics by accident in 1928. He noticed that some kinds of mold prevent bacteria from growing. Researchers later learned that several kinds of single-celled living things can do this. By the 1940s, doctors learned how to use antibiotics to treat diseases.

Antibiotics are usually quite safe. Like other drugs, they sometimes produce bad effects. For example, some people are allergic to penicillin. The drug makes them itch and may make it hard for them to breathe.

See also **disease and sickness; drugs and medicines;** and **Fleming, Sir Alexander.**

antibody

Your body is always on guard against dangerous invaders. If anything enters your body that doesn't belong there, the body immediately starts to fight against it. One important weapon the body uses against invaders is called an antibody. An antibody is a special chemical the body makes to fight and destroy a particular invader.

There are many kinds of invaders that might cause you to get sick. We call these invaders *antigens.* One kind of antigen is a virus that can cause you to catch a cold or the flu. Another kind is the poison in a snake's bite.

When any antigen enters our bodies, special cells called *lymphocytes* notice it and send out an alarm. Some lymphocytes immediately begin to make antibodies designed to fight the particular invader. There is one kind of antibody for each particular antigen. At any moment, antibodies in our bodies are fighting one invader or another.

Most of the time, we feel healthy because antibodies are winning their battles. Sometimes there may be too many invaders,

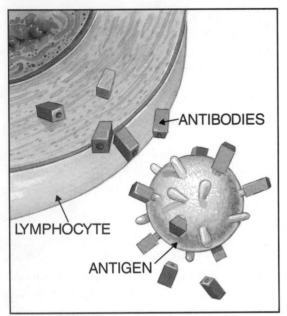

The antibodies (rectangle shapes) are made to fasten onto the enemy antigen (round shape) and kill it.

and they get a chance to multiply in our bodies. Then we get sick. Sometimes, we need medicine to help kill the invaders. Once the antibodies catch up and start to win again, we begin to get better.

Our bodies are best at making antibodies for invaders that have been there before. Some diseases, such as measles, you can get only once. After that, your body can make measles antibodies quickly. The measles virus will never be able to make you sick again. We say you are *immune* to measles.

You can avoid getting some diseases by being *vaccinated.* This means you are given a weak dose of a virus or a bacterium—not enough to make you sick, but enough to alert the lymphocytes. They go to work to make the right antibodies to kill the disease-causing germs. If the virus or bacterium tries to invade your body later, the antibodies are ready—they attack the enemy and destroy it.

Sometimes, antibodies attack when we don't want them to. Doctors learned in the 1800s that there are four basic types of blood. They are called A, B, AB, and O. If you have type A blood, you cannot have a trans-

fusion of type O blood. Antibodies will attack the "foreign" blood and destroy it. Antibodies also attack a transplanted heart or kidney. People who receive transplants must take special medicines to keep the antibodies from destroying their new organs.

See also **disease and sickness.**

Antigua, *see* West Indies

---

antihistamine, *see* allergy

---

antiseptic

An antiseptic is a chemical that kills germs. Antiseptics can help prevent illnesses and infections.

Strong antiseptics called *disinfectants* are used for cleaning in homes, stores, and hospitals. They are in household bleach and other cleaning products that kill germs in toilets, bathtubs, and sinks. Many of them are poisonous and can burn the skin. *CAUTION: Never use these antiseptics unless a grown-up is helping you.*

Germs can enter the body through any break in the skin. When germs grow and multiply in a cut, they cause an infection. Doctors put medical antiseptics on serious cuts or other injuries. They also use antiseptics before and after an operation. They wash their hands with special antiseptic soap, and they use antiseptics on the patient's skin where the operation will take place.

Until doctors learned to use antiseptics, most people who had an operation died afterward of infections. In the 1800s, doctors discovered that antiseptics could prevent these infections. Since then, operations have been much safer.

Many families keep antiseptic ointments for small cuts or scratches. Some doctors say that these antiseptics are not really necessary. If you have a cut or scratch, a good treatment is to wash it with soap and water and cover it with a clean bandage.